THE GENTLEM

Born and brought up in New Delhi, 16-year-old Ayush Ansal has travelled across the world and is currently studying in Gordonstoun, Scotland. An avid guitarist, he believes that his emphasis on dedication and determination has led to him being able to balance the demands of academics with other interests. He has always been fascinated with writing stories and this represents his first serious attempt at writing a novel.

To pretty boy his Damn you're smart.

From

THE GENTLEMEN OF
FINANCE

Ayush Ansal

RUPA

Published by
Rupa Publications India Pvt. Ltd 2013
7/16, Ansari Road, Daryaganj
New Delhi 110002

Sales centres:
Allahabad Bengaluru Chennai
Hyderabad Jaipur Kathmandu
Kolkata Mumbai

ISBN: 978-81-291-2376-3

10 9 8 7 6 5 4 3 2 1

The moral right of the author has been asserted.

Typeset in Minion Pro 11/14.5

Printed at Thomson Press India Ltd., Faridabad

To the 1960s,
for giving me the greatest music collection
I could have asked for.

Contents

Contents

Welcome to the Jungle

Nortigo was a city of darkness and brooding industrial wealth. Within all of its winding streets and copper alleys, it bloomed as a shadow and watched menacingly the grassy plains of England that surrounded it. Divided by a river into two halves, the rich had conquered the upper city while the poor fought to survive in the lower. Nested halfway between London and the city of Rye, Nortigo was a void of shade that had originally been a small woodland town, but after years of black-market economic boom, it was now something completely different and unendingly more sinister.

In one of the many structures that inhabited the city, William Mulligan sat back in his chair and stared at the smoke emanating from the minimal flame that burned at the opposite end of his cigarette. He was dressed in a beige suit with a pink silk shirt that perfectly complimented his tan and muscular upper body. His hair was pulled straight back and the comb lines remained confidently visible. Mostly concealed behind his shirt, on his upper left arm, there was a tattoo, which read 'Sympathy for the Devil'. Upon seeing him for the first time, people seemed to perceive him more as a hot-headed Mafioso than his true persona, which was something much more coldly delicate yet infinitely more lethal.

A golden nameplate on Mulligan's office table read, *Head of Regional Operations* and it was placed in a prominent fashion. It was a gentle yet constant reminder that aside from his casual attitude, Mulligan really was the regional boss of the Royal Citizen's Bank. The rest of his table consisted of sparsely populated documents, a few pens and a silver ashtray that already had grey mounds of ash and stubs in it. The floor was covered with a furry black carpet that was soft enough to comfortably sleep on while the walls were of a bright white colour. Behind the man who occupied the room was a large window that provided a magnificent view of the metropolitan city and currently served as the only light source illuminating the chamber.

Across Mulligan was a grand double glass door with wood panelling and it was observed carefully by the sole occupant of the room as he inhaled a final drag from his cigarette.

The phone buzzed and interrupted the absolute silence that the man had come to cherish and enjoy.

Mulligan stubbed his finished cigarette into the ashtray and tapped the blinking red button on his phone. 'Jimmy is here to see you, sir,' said the soft efficient voice of Mulligan's secretary from the other end. 'Send him in,' replied Mulligan, without thinking twice, and moments later the glass door to the office swung open and a polished young man entered.

James Wolfenstein or 'Jimmy' was a wunderkind when it came to numbers. Mulligan had quickly identified the young man's potential and hired him. The kid had a child-like charm that went perfectly with his slender physique and his shiny blond hair. People around the office had quickly seen that he was not someone mature enough to carry a strong name like James Wolfenstein, which originated from his German heritage, and had quickly and politely nicknamed him 'Jimmy'; plain and simple.

Jimmy entered Mulligan's office wearing his usual navy blue suit with a shiny clean white shirt. He nervously met his boss's eyes and then counted the number of cigarettes in the ashtray. Five. 'Boss, with all due respect, you have got to cut back on the tobacco.' Jimmy had maintained a frank and comfortable relationship with his boss and this was reflected in the way he spoke. 'Jimmy, I promise you, I'll stop smoking the day I die,' joked Mulligan in response and both men let out a cheeky and understanding smile.

'So what's on the docket today?' asked Mulligan, as he considered another cigarette.

'Well I checked with your secretary and she said you don't have any meetings this morning so I thought that maybe you could have a look at this pair of potential clients.' Jimmy was quick with his response and Mulligan wondered if the matter needed quick attention.

'What's the potential?' asked Mulligan coldly, as he addictively fingered the box of cigarettes in his left pant pocket.

Jimmy took a breath and glossed over a sheet of paper that he had pulled out from his jacket pocket. He quickly took in the important details so that he could make a quick detailed presentation to his boss. 'Well, the client would officially be a small corporate called Dunham Clothing and Garments. It's owned and run by two brothers. They're doing fairly well and seem to be looking for financial backing to expand. From the information I have, it seems as though the figure would be around half a million.'

Mulligan absorbed the information and asked, 'Investment or loan?'

Jimmy immediately felt like a naive person for stupidly missing out such a critical detail. 'Loan,' he responded solemnly.

Mulligan nodded and asked a further question, 'Why are we going to them? Why aren't they coming to us?'

Jimmy saw that his boss had picked up his lead and let out a soft smile of satisfaction. He then continued and restrained himself from getting too excited as he shared the next juicy detail about the possible proposition, 'Well, apparently they already signed with Brookstone Bank, but my source tells me that Brookstone lost the paperwork and now the Dunham brothers are being unpleasant during the re-negotiations.'

Mulligan smiled. That's all he needed to hear. Brookstone Bank had been a longterm rival for him. He would never let an easy opportunity like this go to waste.

'There's no time to spare,' Mulligan's voice was commanding as he continued to speak, 'I'm going to go talk to the Dunham brothers right now. We can't let this chance go to waste.' Mulligan got up from his chair and walked around the table, revealing his brown leather shoes to Jimmy who eyed them with appreciation. He admired his boss's amazing sense of style.

Mulligan checked his pockets for his essentials: wallet, phone and cigarettes and then asked Jimmy, 'Where are they staying and what are their names?'

Jimmy once again glanced at his sheet of information and said, 'Mark Dunham and Peter Dunham. Both single. They're staying at the Great Marina Hotel. I couldn't get their room numbers though.'

Mulligan nodded. He was satisfied with the amount of information that Jimmy had obtained, but realized that some of his other employees could have easily done better. Mulligan knew that the kid was adept at crunching numbers and bureaucracy, but sometimes he wished for Jimmy to be just a little bit more street smart.

Leaving Jimmy behind in his office, Mulligan walked past his secretary and through the grand service lobby of his bank. The interior of the Royal Citizen's Bank was a palette of refined Italian marble and bulletproof glass. As Mulligan quickly walked past dozens of customers, dressed in everything from black suits to beachwear, he was constantly addressed with phrases such as, 'Good morning, boss' and 'Hello sir' from his employees. As pleasant as these greetings were, they occasionally seemed to prevent him from doing his job as efficiently as possible.

Mulligan finally reached the awe-inspiring entrance to his place of work and paced down the spaced staircase that led to the porch. The valet saw him approaching and quickly signalled to the chauffeur waiting around a bend. Moments later, Mulligan's car pulled up in front and the driver got out and held the door open for him.

Mulligan slid into the back of his Cadillac Sixteen, which then quickly revved to life with a powerful growl from the engine. The chauffeur was a short man with a stout body and a pale white skin tone. His teeth, however, were impeccable and Mulligan once again noticed this as he flashed a smile and asked, 'Where to boss?'

'Great Marina Hotel.'

Mulligan hit the button on the door and the window automatically rolled down. He then lit a cigarette and blew smoke out the window, after every lengthy drag, as he watched the tall buildings and countless villa-like residences of Nortigo whiz by. As the car circled around into the poorer part of the city, Mulligan observed the crumbling homes and broken cars of the narcotic-enslaved and poverty stricken people that made up a significant part of the population of the city. From the comfort of his limited edition concept car, the world outside felt like something distant and unreal. Having grown up in an upper middle income family, he had never been exposed to much financial hardship or even restraint.

The journey once again led back to the richer and more comforting part of the city and Mulligan's thoughts shifted onto what was going to happen soon. He thought about any preparations that he should make and came to the conclusion that the only thing he would need would be one of his most powerful tools: his business card.

The car came to a smooth halt at what Mulligan had come to appreciate as one of the grandest entrances to a building in the world. The car stood on a smooth tar road, which did not have a single tyre mark on it. To the left a black marble waterfall, in the form of a gargantuan man, blocked out the view of the rest of the city, creating an exquisitely charming surrounding essence. The water from the waterfall dropped over forty feet, but barely made any sound because of the mechanical genius behind it. To the left was the real treat: the actual entrance to the Great Marina Hotel. The building itself was a massive structure, fifteen floors high, and about seven acres large. It was of a beige colour and conveyed a colosseum-like grandness.

Mulligan exited his car and walked into the hotel. The lobby perfectly matched the rest of the building, with a black patterned floor, sparsely placed seating, a small fountain in the center, the reception and concierge to the right and the coffee shop entrance to the left. Mulligan smiled, a wide smile revealing his shiny and perfect white teeth, and approached a woman at the reception.

'Hey Julie,' he spoke in a suave voice as he attempted to charm the efficient-looking woman, in uniform, across him.

'Hello Mr Mulligan,' she replied shyly. They both already knew each other as Mulligan had used her countless times to get things done within the hotel. He did, however, always reward her with compensation of course.

'Point me in the direction of the Dunham brothers, will you?' Mulligan asked softly, as he withdrew a fifty dollar bill from his wallet.

Julie saw the bill coming out of Mulligan's wallet and replied, 'They're eating lunch in the coffee shop.'

Mulligan smiled once again and passed her the money. Julie picked it up and nodded in acknowledgement. Bribes were one of the core factors for doing smooth business.

A few moments later, Mulligan had once again crossed the impressive lobby and was now standing in the coffee shop, hopelessly attempting to identify the Dunham brothers. He had thought that it would be easy to spot two men eating lunch alone in a family restaurant, but it was clear that he had underestimated the number of business lunches that might be taking place.

It was a relief when the maître d' approached Mulligan and waited for him to say something. Once again Mulligan drew out a fifty dollar bill and then placed it in the maître d's hand. 'Point me to the Dunham party, please.' Mulligan's request was quickly fulfilled as he was escorted, through the busy restaurant, to a table where he saw two annoyed looking men sipping beers and waiting for their meals.

Mark Dunham was dressed in beige pants and a blue half-sleeve t-shirt, which was tucked in. His flaky blonde hair was parted to one side and his plain black shoes stood out against the purple floor carpet of the restaurant. Peter Dunham, on the other hand, was dressed in a full black suit with a black shirt. Mulligan was unable to estimate their height as they were sitting down, but both looked seemingly tall.

'You must be Mark and Peter Dunham,' said Mulligan as he flashed a big smile and saw the two men study him.

'Who are you?' barked Peter rudely, in return.

'My name is William Mulligan and I head the Royal Citizen's Bank in this great city,' Mulligan continued to speak proudly as he watched the interest of the men he was talking to escalate, 'I am aware that you are currently re-negotiating with Brookstone Bank after their little stupidity and want you to know that it is not wise to get into business with incapable establishments. I am here to tell you that if you are willing to consider The Royal Citizen's Bank as your financial benefactor, I will personally ensure that you are looked after with the utmost care and treated with the highest authority of respect.'

Mulligan knew what he was doing. After the debacle with Brookstone, these men were looking for respect and attention rather than just someone to take a loan from. They knew their business was going well and getting financial backing wouldn't be a problem, they just wanted someone who actually respected them as business associates. Mulligan didn't actually respect them. They were still a very small establishment. But he definitely wasn't going to tell them that.

The Dunham brothers were supremely interested and immediately liked the idea of switching banks. Mulligan drew two business cards from his jacket pocket and handed one to each of the brothers. His business card was absolutely perfect. He had spent hours agonizing over little details and it was clear that it had paid off. The font was attractive, yet not distracting.

The ink was both prominent, yet long lasting. The thickness was a little more than usual and a slight strafing of the paper created a unique background pattern.

'Let's set up a meeting for tomorrow,' said Peter Dunham excitedly.

Mulligan's approach had clearly worked. 'I'll send a car to pick you up at ten tomorrow. Please make sure to let Brookstone know that the deal's off with them, though. We don't want a double contract on our hands now, do we?' Mulligan's tone was half-joking, but everyone understood he was serious.

From the corner of his eye, Mulligan saw a waiter with a tray of food approaching and decided it was time to leave. 'Well, it's time for me to go. Enjoy your lunch.' He then turned around and left the restaurant.

Ten minutes later, Mulligan was once again riding in his unnaturally luxurious car through the wide roads of the city. His hand held a lit cigarette and grey fumes of nicotine and tobacco coursed through his lungs. He pulled out his phone and called Jimmy.

'What's up boss?' asked Jimmy, almost instantly, as he answered the call.

'I talked to the Dunham brothers. It went well. They're going to be coming in tomorrow, so prep the paperwork and keep conference room seven booked.' Mulligan's tone was emotionless, but he could feel Jimmy's excitement on the other end.

'Nice going boss!'

Mulligan smiled and asked, 'Now that I'm all the way uptown, is there anything else here that I can take care of?'

The pressing of keyboard keys echoed through the phone

as Jimmy searched through his computer and broke the otherwise complete vocal silence.

Jimmy muttered unsurely, 'We need to send a "reminder" to someone uptown, but I don't think that's your kind of thing, boss. Don't take me the wrong way, you definitely have the physical ability to do it, but you might not want to get your hands dirty for no reason.'

Ah, the 'reminder'. More often than not, people with bad debts failed to stay in regular contact with their respective banking institutions and, in extreme cases, these people had to be sent unpleasant 'reminders'. A 'reminder' would usually consist of some form of temporary bodily harm to be inflicted onto the offender so that he would be 'reminded' to pay up his debts or surrender collateral.

Mulligan scoffed and said, 'Come on kid. I've been giving "reminders" for as long as I can remember and I actually, kind of, enjoy putting the occasional scumbag in place.'

'Okay boss,' answered Jimmy unsurely, 'The guy's name is Andrew Cobb. He missed a return payment of ten grand this month. I'll send your driver the address.'

Mulligan hung up.

The drive from the hotel to the Cobb residence was less than five minutes. It was a small and unimpressive house. The white paint was peeling off the walls and the door was completely scratched. Even the grass and plants had died. It seemed like the place had been hit by a twister. No wonder Mr Cobb here had taken a loan for home improvement. Mulligan carefully walked to the entrance. He didn't want to step on anything that would spoil his shoes.

A bell was placed on the wall next to the door and Mulligan pressed it. An unpleasant loud chime occurred throughout the house and after a few moments, the door swung open. Andrew Cobb was a disgusting man.

Cobb wore a stained wife-beater and a pair of red boxer shorts. He was about five feet ten inches tall and skinny to the bone. A disgusting smell of excreta and beer surrounded him and his messy hair and brown teeth only made him that much more repulsive.

Mulligan grabbed the hideous man by the neck and threw him onto the pavement in one quick motion. Cobb was completely taken aback by this seemingly unprovoked attack and attempted to figure out what was happening. Mulligan placed his foot against the back of Cobb's head and pushed his face onto the uneven floor. Just enough pressure was applied to cause pain, but not enough actually to scratch the man's face.

'Who the hell are you?' screamed Cobb, at what he perceived to be a psychopath.

'I'm William Mulligan. Royal Citizen's Bank.' His tone was cold and vengeful.

'Look, I'll pay back the money next month!' barked Cobb defensively.

Mulligan lit a cigarette, took three drags and then stubbed it out on Cobb's hideously hairy back.

'What the hell are you doing?' screeched Cobb as the pain from the cigarette burn grew steadily.

'Here's what we are going to do okay? You are going to pay the ten grand by tomorrow. If you don't, I'm going to come back again and again until you pay up. If you can't come up with the money by the end of the week, I'm going to take everything you own. You won't even have underwear that you can call your own. Got that?'

Mulligan wasn't bluffing.

Cobb let a tear shed and Mulligan knew that his point had been conveyed. He released his foot from the back of the man's head and walked away.

Back at the office, Mulligan sat resting in his chair and measured the success of the day's events. After a swift overview, he knew things couldn't have gone better. Satisfied with himself, he let a smile slip, but his thoughts were quickly interrupted by the buzzing of his phone. He tapped the button and was greeted by his secretary's voice, 'I have Mr Dover on the phone for you, sir.'

Mulligan's smile quickly dissipated as he heard the name of the man that he regarded as his nemesis. Benjamin Dover was the head of the Brookstone Bank in the city and had maintained a constant struggle for greater market share with Mulligan for a number of years.

'Put him through,' said Mulligan reluctantly.

A few moments later, Dover's husky voice burst through the phone, 'You know you really are a piece of work, Mulligan. You're stealing clients now? Have you really stooped that low?'

Mulligan grew angry and responded with hostility, 'Don't act like you wouldn't have done the same thing. You dropped the ball Dover and that comes with repercussions.'

'The Dunham brothers were my clients! You had no right to...'

Mulligan cut the call. He was in no mood to get into a fruitless argument about who held the higher moral ground.

A few minutes later, Mulligan's eyes hovered over his gold-plated watch and he saw that it was time to go home. Even though he enjoyed his work, he knew it was critical to get some rest so that he would be able to perform at his best the next day.

The drive from the office to his home was a solemn one. The night had taken over the day and the excessive pollution from the city ensured the absolute invisibility of the stars. The crescent moon that stood in bright contrast against the sky seemed to be the only source of natural light flooding the surface.

The car took one last swerve and stood waiting against a massive bronze gate that had the sign 'Park Woods' sprawled across it. To the right of the gate was a small guardhouse, which served as a small security room. A man dressed in a blue and white uniform exited the small structure and walked toward the car. Mulligan noticed that this was some new kid and hence could not recognize him. Agonizingly, he reached into the back pocket of the seat and drew out some necessary paperwork. The guard knocked on the glass and Mulligan rolled down the window. After noticing him more closely, the kid appeared older than he seemed earlier.

'Good evening, sir. May I know where you're headed?' the Kid Guard's voice was unsure.

Mulligan scoffed and replied, 'To my house.'

The Kid Guard smiled at the cheeky reply and asked again, 'What's your address sir?'

'138 Park Woods,' replied Mulligan in a cold voice.

The Kid Guard pulled out a small printed sheet of paper and glanced through it. Upon finding what he was looking for, he asked, 'Ah, Mr Mulligan. Can I have your security word please?'

Mulligan glanced at his own sheet of paper and replied, 'Swordfish.'

Without saying anything and only acknowledging the response with a nod, the Kid Guard walked back to the guard booth and hit a large red button. The electronically operated gates swiftly swung open and the car sped through.

Park Woods was the epitome of luxury residential housing. The area in itself was about one hundred acres and had sprawling trees everywhere. The roads were ridiculously eight-lane wide and each house was designed keeping in mind the public image of its owner. After a three-minute drive through the area, the car arrived at Mulligan's private estate.

The home of William Mulligan seemed more like an exquisite piece of art than a physical structure. Its design was a reflection of a traditional manor or castle with an obscene amount of wooden flooring and brooding walls. The eight-bedroom home was ridden with leather furniture and two private fireplaces. The front section was home to a large yard that served as a pleasant sight to those driving into the house while the small open space behind the house consisted of a medium sized pool, a hot-tub and a sauna. For such a large home, some might say that it was almost pitiful that it had only one resident. What they didn't know, however, was that William Mulligan was a man who embraced solitude.

After a quick shower, Mulligan changed into his bathrobe and headed down to his study. He descended a large twirling staircase that would be familiar to anyone who had been to the opera. His study was a large room that focused all of its attention onto a royal desk that sat in the center. Mulligan took a seat behind the desk then drew out his ashtray and placed it on the table.

Cigarette in hand, Mulligan shoved aside some loans that he had planned to look over and decided to place a call to a 'special' friend of his instead. He dialled the number and enjoyed the tobacco in his body as he waited, listening to the monotone of the dialing phone.

A few moments later, the phone was answered.

There was silence for a few moments as both waited to listen for the click that told them that the phone was being tapped. When there was none, Mulligan spoke first, 'Roger, it's Mulligan here.'

'Ah! Mr Mulligan! Good to hear from you! So what can I do for my favourite customer today? Maybe you want to put some money on some street races? The odds are really good!' Roger's voice was unnaturally ecstatic.

'Nah Roger, I was actually hoping to get in on the big baseball game tomorrow. I want to put five grand on the regional team.'

Mulligan heard as Roger filled out an entry in his register.

'It's done. Anything else?' asked Roger. Mulligan was a big player when it came to betting and he didn't want to let any chance go to waste, now that he had him on the phone.

'Nope, that's all.'

The call ended. Roger was unhappy that Mulligan had only put down one small bet and promised himself to try harder next time.

Next morning, Mulligan got up at exactly 9:03 a.m. and twenty seven minutes later, he was dressed and in the car. The Cadillac sped through the city and three cigarettes later, Mulligan pulled up in front of the Royal Citizen's Bank.

He got out and paced up the stairs as he nodded in acknowledgement to whoever wished him a 'Good morning'. Upon entering the lobby, he was surprised as he saw that the only customer in the bank was screaming at a teller. The man was dressed in a red shirt and beige pants with a fedora and a shiny fake gold watch. The teller he was yelling at was clearly extremely upset and Mulligan felt blood pump into his fists.

Even though he would like to punch the petty-looking man, he made the rational decision and indicated for two guards to grab him and bring him up to his office instead.

Ten minutes later, Mulligan sat in his office, with a cigarette in his mouth, and his eyes studying the man across him. The man in the red shirt had been no match for the bank's guards, and even though he had resisted in the beginning, he had stopped all attempts to free himself after he saw a loaded Beretta in each of their pocket holsters.

'What's your name?' asked Mulligan with cold hostility.

'Jerry,' replied the man.

'Your full name,' clarified Mulligan.

'Jerome Helter.'

'Okay, answer me this Jerome,' Mulligan was a stupid remark away from breaking the man's nose, 'Why the hell were you screaming at my employee?'

Helter flashed a smug look and fired back, 'I have an account here and she wasn't letting me withdraw any cash.'

Mulligan took a puff, studied his opponent and then buzzed his secretary, 'Send that teller up, please.'

Minutes passed as both men watched each other with cold unflinching eyes.

A pretty-looking teller walked into the office and flashed a look of disgust as she saw Jerome seated across her boss.

Mulligan smiled at his attractive employee and asked, 'Why didn't you let this man here withdraw any money dear?'

The teller took a deep breath and replied as calmly as she could, 'He has already made three withdrawals this week. That's the maximum for a savings account.'

Mulligan took a breath from his cigarette and watched Jerome's face drop. He clearly knew he was wrong. 'Take the day off dear,' Mulligan told the teller, who quickly thanked him and left the office.

Waiting for Mulligan to say something, Jerome began to sweat.

'Now listen to me scumbag; you're never going to come back here again. You understand? You want to make any further withdrawals, use an ATM or go to another branch. Now get out.' Mulligan had been exceedingly cold.

The man quickly got up and scurried out of the office, cursing himself for messing up. Mulligan knew he had done the right thing and wondered if he had done anything wrong. His self-doubt was quickly tarnished however, as he took another drag from his cigarette.

Ten minutes later, Mulligan put out his cigarette and picked up his phone. The direct line to his secretary was clear and he asked, 'Are the Dunham brothers here yet?' The secretary put the call on mute and inquired about the situation, while Mulligan waited and stared at the remainders of his most recent cigarette.

'Yes, they are sir; they're waiting in conference room seven.'

'Good, tell Jimmy to meet me there.'

Mulligan put down the receiver and began the short walk from his office to his favourite room of the building; conference room seven.

CR: 7 was the perfect place to conduct any sort of business. The soundproof room with its leather black chairs and cushiony walls provided a safe yet comfortable environment for everyone. The fact that one of the glass windows provided a magnificent view of the city furthered the positive impact of the room. The only shortcoming was that it could only hold a maximum of eight people. This, however, also seemed to work in Mulligan's favour sometimes, as meetings were much more efficient with a smaller and more core group of business associates.

Upon entering, Mulligan found that Jimmy, the Dunham brothers and another man were already waiting. Jimmy flashed a big smile and the paperwork in front of him assured Mulligan that the contract was ready. Mulligan recognized the other new man in the room as a contract-efficiency specialist lawyer and it was clear that he was here representing the Dunham brothers.

Everyone shook hands and then sat down.

The specialist lawyer spoke first and Mulligan instantly didn't like it, 'My name is Duane Crow and I'm here representing the Dunham brothers. I would like to make it clear that if a mishap, like the one at Brookstone, takes place, you will be heavily liable.'

Mulligan smiled reassuringly and said, 'Jimmy here already has the paperwork prepped and we want you to know that this deal is going down smoother than whiskey.'

The Dunham brothers nodded approvingly as Jimmy passed around the contract.

The lawyer quickly went through the proposition and spoke again, 'You're driving a hard bargain, you know?'

Mulligan opened his mouth to respond, but Jimmy went first, 'We're running a bank here. What are we going to do? Reduce interest rates? You know we can't do that.'

The lawyer spoke again, much more smoothly this time, 'That I understand. I was, however, indicating towards the other fringe benefits.'

The Dunham brothers looked at their lawyer with approval and both Jimmy and Mulligan noticed that these guys were pushing too hard. Mulligan, however, didn't want to let

Brookstone have the satisfaction of winning back a client and came up with a sufficient proposition.

'The first month becomes interest free and we'll bump up your overdraft period by a week.'

Everyone nodded their approval. Mulligan then decided to add the finishing touch.

'We'll also pick up the hotel bill.'

The Dunham brothers let out wide grins of satisfaction and the contract was quickly signed. It had been a smooth deal.

Soldier in Our Town

A large audience gathered around a massive podium in front of a brand new building. The building was made almost completely out of glass and a large black sign above the fourteenth floor read 'IXL Bank'. The opening of the third and the newest competitor in the banking sector of the city had attracted almost everyone who was even remotely linked to the finance sector to the extravagant opening ceremony.

Businessmen from every corner of the city had come to broker deals and look for opportunities to exploit the bank before it began business and many of them had already spotted the abundant chances that they would have. The IXL Head Office had clearly rushed the project and the administration was fumbling and falling in every direction. Adverts for jobs ran rampant and trustworthy employees were at a minimum.

'Good morning, Ladies and Gentlemen. Welcome to the big launch of the brand new IXL Bank!' The man hosting the opening event was clearly attempting to get the crowd excited about the ceremony, but since the people attending mostly consisted of those who were not too happy about the opening, there was only silence. Not even applause.

Quickly getting over his failed opening statement, and realizing the mood of the attendees, the announcer decided to skip the jokes and quips he had prepared and head straight to the ribbon cutting ceremony.

'To inaugurate the opening of one of the greatest financial institutions in the world, we will have the mayor of the city cut the ribbon and open the doors to the excited customers who have lined up around the corner.'

Benjamin Dover, who sat in the very first row, and had a good view of everything, let out a little chuckle as he heard what the announcer had to say. The mayor was an old pig who had no real power in the city. Everyone knew that the banks and the mob were what really kept the place from falling apart. Hearing that apparent 'customers' had lined up to get into the bank, Dover turned his head to the right. He saw nothing but a couple of hoodlums looking to extort a little money, from whatever buffoon was in charge, and a small company of actors attempting to portray civilians who were excitedly awaiting the opening of the doors.

In what world do people get in line for the opening of a bank? Especially some third grade bank like IXL? These people clearly have no idea as to who their targeted consumer market is. Dover simply could not comprehend as to how any of this would help set up a good image for the bank. Anyone with half an interest in finance knew that IXL was a failing and backward international firm that had failed to adapt to modern policies and as to why anyone would be impressed by the mayor, was something that Dover would never understand. After all, the opening of the Brookstone Bank was inaugurated by eight different ministers while the Royal Citizen's Bank had the CEOs of sixty-four of the Fortune 500 companies attending. This, in comparison, was an absolute joke.

Mulligan sat in the lounge of The Royal Citizen's Bank

Regional Office and watched the opening of IXL on the sixty inch flat screen in front of him. He was comfortably settled on a couch with his feet up and his head leaning on a cushion against the arm rest. Behind him was a glowing sign that prominently stated 'No Smoking' and in his hand he held a cigarette.

The fact that he was alone quickly changed as Jimmy strolled into the room without knocking and was surprised to see his boss.

'Boss, you can't smoke in here,' murmured Jimmy, just a second before realizing that he might have made a mistake.

Mulligan let out a suave smile and said, 'No Jimmy, I'm not allowed to smoke in here. But I am going to. Do you know why?'

Taken aback by the entrapping question, Jimmy phrased his response as safely as he could, 'Because you're the boss?'

Mulligan smiled and nodded.

Jimmy turned around and saw that Mulligan was watching the opening ceremony on the humongous television. Jimmy already knew what the news was, but this was the first time that he was seeing the building. Mulligan stubbed out the cigarette on the white marble floor and lit another one.

'What do you think kid?' asked Mulligan.

Jimmy looked at his boss, hoping to get some sort of hint as to what kind of response he wanted. Deciding that Mulligan had the best poker-face he had ever seen, he gave up and answered honestly, 'The Bank's not going to survive. No chance. But even though it is eventually going to fail, we must hope to minimalize the damage that it can cause during the short time that it does play the role of our competitor.'

Mulligan chuckled and Jimmy tried to understand why.

'Listen, kid,' Mulligan started speaking in a matter-of-fact tone, 'IXL's a joke. The bank itself isn't even fully staffed yet. Also, I made a call upstairs and they told me that IXL is going to hold a meeting in thirty days as to whether they want to actually seriously start up the bank or cut some minor losses and make a big bag of money by selling the building off as residential or maybe even commercial space, if they can swing the licence.'

'So depending on how well the bank does in the first month, they're going to decide as to whether they want to shut it down or not?' Jimmy asked as he attempted to confirm that he had understood what was going on, correctly.

'Exactly,' replied his boss, confirming that he had grasped the concept.

Jimmy watched on television as the tired and resented old mayor stumbled onto the podium in a shabby suit with faded shoes and cut the ribbon. He then turned to Mulligan who he saw had stubbed out his second cigarette and was now on his third.

'Jimmy, I've been thinking about this for the past two days and as you know that I am a man who doesn't like uncertainty, I have come to a rather interesting decision.'

Not having the slightest idea as to what his boss was ranting off about, Jimmy continued to listen attentively.

Mulligan handed Jimmy the morning's newspaper with an advert circled and continued speaking, 'As you can see from the newspaper advertisement, IXL is looking for Loan Associates. The fact that they're not promoting internally, and are willing to leave their entire cash flow to newly-hired men is something that perfectly reflects their stupidity and is a mistake that they're going to pay for dearly.'

Jimmy's interest peaked.

Mulligan continued, 'It's time for us to start a not-so-legal project. You and two other men, who I have yet to pick, are going to resign from this bank and take up jobs as Loan Executives at IXL. Then, I want you to give out as many bad loans as you can so that by the end of the month IXL has no other option but to sell off the building. At the end of this endeavour, you will have your jobs waiting for you with a little extra bonus on the side. I know it sounds extremely dangerous and far-fetched, but the truth is that you're going to be doing everyone a favour. IXL will probably make a lot of money from the sale, our bank and Brookstone will have an easier life looking for clients and even the government won't have to set aside valuable taxpayer money to bail out the stupid bank when it would inevitably fail.'

The room fell silent for a few minutes and the only sound that could be heard was the voice of the announcer still pitifully attempting to rally a passion-dead crowd through the television.

After a few moments of deep thought, Jimmy finally spoke, 'I'll do it. But only on one condition.'

'Which is?' asked Mulligan thoughtfully.

'I get to pick the men who come with me on this little…. adventure.'

Mulligan let out a chuckle and replied, 'I wouldn't have it any other way.'

Jimmy got up and departed, leaving Mulligan with a lot to think about. If this worked out, he would have hit a home run and everyone was going to get bumped up. If this didn't, however, the repercussions would be great for those involved.

In his medium-sized yet extremely technological office,

Jimmy sat going through a list of six names he had come up with. These six people were the only ones who he thought he could trust enough to stick with to the end. They were the only ones who would not only be open to a little corporate espionage, but would welcome it.

That, however, wasn't enough. Jimmy had to ensure that these people were not going to crack under pressure or go to the flatfoots. These people had to stick to their guns to the end, and give everything they had, to make sure that IXL would not last more than a month.

After another thirty minutes of consideration and looking over files and reports, Jimmy cut out one name. He then got up from his seat, took a deep breath of confidence and headed to Mulligan's office.

A buzz from his secretary, and a knock on the door, informed Mulligan that he had a visitor. Then the door swung open and Jimmy strolled in with an impactful smile that only caused Mulligan to light yet another cigarette in reaction.

'You got anything for me kid?' asked Mulligan as his eyes hovered over the concealed piece of paper in Jimmy's grasp.

'The names of the people I'm considering for the infiltration. I don't know any of them well and I think it should be you who picks the two out of these five,' said Jimmy as he handed Mulligan the list.

A moment passed, and cigarette smoke took over the air as Mulligan went over every name. After deep consideration, he finally revealed his judgment, 'Joseph Garrett and Eugene Dime. The others are either too square or too bent.'

Jimmy nodded in unsure response.

'You don't like my decision wonder-boy?' asked Mulligan sarcastically.

'It's just that, I was pretty sure about Adam Greene. He's our type of man,' Jimmy appealed innocently.

Mulligan took a deep breath and replied, 'Adam Greene is a low level accounts guy. I know you two got close when you started working here, but he really isn't the type of guy to get involved with this type of activity. Remember kid, when it comes to business, leave your feelings home for your wife and kids.'

Quickly realizing what his boss was trying to convey, Jimmy nodded understandingly and then left the office.

An hour later, Jimmy sat in his office with Joseph Garrett and Eugene Dime across him. The fact that he had called this urgent meeting only ten minutes ago and had received such an efficient response helped Jimmy to maintain strong faith in Mulligan's decision.

Joe Garrett and Eugene Dime both came off as typical office workers; unmarried men around the age of twenty-five who often played golf on weekends and went to the pub every day after work. Neither of them had any apparent distinguishing features and that ensured that they wouldn't have trouble blending in.

Garrett had pitch-black hair that was pulled back. He wore a beige suit with a white shirt. Dime, on the other hand, had an exquisite fashion sense and was wearing a well-cut black suit with a light maroon shirt and black leather shoes.

'So what's going on Jim?' Garrett asked his colleague. He was clearly unaware of why the meeting had been called, and judging from the look on Dime's face, Jimmy was sure that he was as clueless as his friend.

'You have been chosen by some men, at the high points of the ladder, for a rather irregular task.' As usual, Jimmy attempted to maintain a sense of intrigue by phrasing his sentences extremely elegantly, 'If you do decide to join me and take up this opportunity, we will make more money in a single month than we do in five years, otherwise.'

Dime who was clearly beginning to see the cracks, spoke demandingly, 'Just give it to us straight.'

'The three of us take up jobs as Loan Execs at IXL, give out a bunch of bum loans for the one month we're there. Then once the place shuts down we come back to our jobs here and find three big fancy suitcases, full of cash, waiting for us. Sounds good?'

Dime and Garrett looked at each other in disbelief and then looked back at Jimmy who maintained his 'this is real' expression. Clearly, this was something that neither of them had been accustomed to earlier.

'And this is sanctioned from upstairs?' asked Garrett unsurely.

'It was their idea, Mulligan's the one who's doing all the pushing and pulling, though.' Jimmy knew that it was essential to let Dime and Garrett think that the head office was in on this. It would increase their chances of going through with it.

'How much exactly are we looking at?' asked Dime sharply.

Jimmy scribbled down a figure on a yellow sheet of paper and passed it across the table. Both Dime and Garrett counted the zeroes twice before looking back up at Jimmy and nodding with definite approval.

Jimmy let out a wide grin as he leaned back in his chair. The game was on.

The next morning Jimmy, Dime and Garrett stood on the porch of the Royal Citizen's Bank dressed in their finest worksuits. A dark green Jaguar pulled up and the valet held the three doors open as the men got in. Jimmy rode shotgun.

The drive was relatively short and quiet, and fortunately enough for the three men, the unknown driver didn't bother to make small talk. The men simply gazed out of their respective windows and envisioned scenarios in their heads as their destination drew closer.

The car pulled up in front of a ginormous glass cuboid that was called the IXL Bank and the three men got out. Jimmy led the way as they walked over the dirty grey concrete pavement and entered the inside of the glass structure for the first time.

The exterior of the building almost always seemed delightful and pleasant as the glass reflected the lovely blue sky above. The interior, however, was a maze of dark corridors that almost felt as if doom lived within the essence of the building. The trio walked through the grim corridor and passed a pair of young men with fancy cellphones and, finally, entered into an even darker and uglier lobby. As horrific as the sight was, it had been successfully intimidating. 'Confidence to the Customer' certainly wasn't the theme the interior designer was going for.

The men walked through the grizzly lobby, which was bathed in black leather and dark maroon carpeting. They approached a receptionist who awaited them with a smile. Her white shining teeth echoed like beacons of hope in the grim atmosphere. Even though the surrounding area was full of young males and females, jogging around in order to get work done, the receptionist made the three men feel as though they were the only ones there.

'What can I do for you, sir?' she asked with a flicker of an Australian accent in her voice.

'My name is James Wolfenstein and these are my colleagues,

Joseph Garrett and Eugene Dime. We're here for our appointment with Mr Ted Hughes.' Jimmy spoke charmingly in order to gain the unnecessary approval of the pretty receptionist.

'Right this way, sir,' she said after scrolling through the list of appointments on her eleven-inch computer monitor. She led the men through a dense crowd and towards a fancy looking, silver elevator.

She pressed the button and the doors opened, this was followed by the three men cramping into the surprisingly small elevator. 'This will take you straight up,' murmured the receptionist as she hit a button reading '14' on the glass elevator control panel and then bid the three men farewell, with a slight wave of the hand as the doors closed.

The elevator ride was a short one, during which all three men got to enjoy Tchaikovsky's 'Romeo and Juliet,' which was being played through the elevator Public Announcement speaker at a minimal volume.

The doors swung open as their journey ended, and the three men fluttered out into a surprisingly bright hallway. The walls were white, the floor was marble and the sources of natural light were too many to count. Nobody was ready for such a magnificent yet welcome change in scenery.

The men strolled behind one another with Jimmy in the lead, and walked towards what seemed like the grandest office in the building. A small table, belonging to the secretary, occupied the space beside the gleaming white door and a plaque of gold colour read 'Mr Hughes: Head of Regional Operations.'

The secretary greeted the three men with a smile, but wasn't nearly as pretty as the receptionist downstairs.

'Good morning, we have a meeting with Mr Hughes,' said Jimmy gently.

Almost robotically, the secretary asked in return, 'Under what name sir?'

'Wolfenstein, Dime and Garrett,' murmured Jimmy in reply.

The secretary nodded that the appointment had checked out and buzzed her boss through the phone.

In the softest yet clearest whisper she alerted her boss that the men from the Royal Citizen's Bank had arrived and she received precise orders to make them wait for fifteen seconds, before sending them in. In those fifteen seconds, Ted Hughes sprayed breath-freshener in his mouth and hid a bottle of whiskey that had been lying on his table in the cabinet. Some people had tobacco, some had alcohol. But everyone had to release their stress.

Exactly fifteen seconds later, the door swung open and, like an invading army, the three gentlemen marched in and took their seats across the man they had come to meet.

Ted Hughes was an overweight man in his mid-forties. With hair falling and graying and an uncontrollable alcohol addiction, the man was clearly a victim of extreme stress with a heart-attack time bomb waiting to go off. The obvious downhill road that the man was on directly complimented the fact that he was heading IXL, which was also something that was destined to fail.

Sitting in the office, opposite the three men who were supposed to 'bring the bank out of the gutter,' according to his bosses, Ted Hughes was a pitiful sight in a badly fitting yet disgracefully expensive suit and a stained worn-out tie.

'So you're James Wolfenstein, the whiz-kid?' asked Ted Hughes with only the faintest of interest.

'My friends call me Jimmy,' replied Jimmy modestly.

Hughes chuckled and spoke frankly, 'Look guys, IXL's gotten off to a rough start. We don't even have an HR department yet, for god's sake. I'm doing all the recruiting myself. But seeing that three young up-and-comers like you are willing to drop RCB and come here, I can only say that I am very glad that things are beginning to pick up. But, I have to ask, why on earth would you risk high-paying safe jobs for a chance to work here? It doesn't fit.'

The answer to this question had been prepared, and Jimmy spoke with false sincerity, 'We just don't have a future at RCB, Mr Hughes. Everything's full-up. The three of us are a team. We work hard and believe that after we've put in good work and hard time, we deserve a bump up. At RCB, however, we simply don't believe that we're going to get that opportunity.'

Ted Hughes nodded approvingly. He could relate to the fake story that the three men had come up with. 'Okay boys. That makes sense. So let's do this.'

Hughes hit the buzzer on his phone and once he knew that his secretary was listening, he asked, 'Did Legal send up the Priority Three paperwork yet?'

'Yes sir, I just got it,' came the emotion-free reply of the woman on the other end of the phone.

'Okay, bring it in please. Oh, and a couple of pens.' Hughes lifted his finger off the buzzer and the line was cut.

Jimmy, Dime and Garrett waited wordlessly with itchy fingers.

Moments later, the secretary walked in carrying three bundles of sheets and laid them on the table.

'Everything's as agreed upon earlier. I'm sorry for the fourteen per cent salary decrease, but I guess it's made up for by the opportunity to get promoted.' Hughes attempt at making sure that his future employees won't sway was absolutely unnecessary, but the three men nodded understandingly in return anyway.

The ball-pen was quickly used to sign meaningless contracts and minutes later both hard and soft copies were made. It had been unnaturally simple, but Hughes was too mentally exhausted to notice this.

'Welcome aboard guys, my secretary will show you to your brand-new offices,' said Hughes, as he wished that the three men would get out already so that he could return to his whiskey.

'Our pleasure to be here,' replied Dime speaking for the first time, inside the building.

The men left the office and were quickly on the tail of the secretary who led them, through a maze of corridors, towards their respective offices. During this time, Garrett decided to make the previously planned update call to Mulligan.

After a few moments of ringing, Mulligan finally answered, 'How's it going Garrett?'

'We're at the cinema, the film's about to begin.'

The call quickly ended. No need to attract unnecessary attention by having conversations about movies, not more than five seconds after getting your job.

The three brand new employees of IXL Bank finally arrived at their offices and the secretary waved them goodbye and walked off. The three offices were in a direct series and identical in every way. If the offices were of good quality, no one would have cared, but these little boxes of boredom were uglier than anything that the three men had ever seen.

The only furniture were two hard wooden chairs and an unfittingly large desk between them. Clearly the process was that the customers would approach the men in these horrendous offices and then depending on how good or bad their loan strategy was, their application would be accepted or rejected.

Usually, if the plan was good, and the collateral was sufficient, the loan would be passed. But, things were different this time. Jimmy, Dime and Garrett needed to give out as many bad loans as they could so that when the end of the month came, almost none of the people to whom the loan was given would be able to generate the return interest and the bank would fail because of absolute cash flow insolvency; sufficiently brilliant and practical.

After the hour-long lunch break, the receptionist finally started to divert customers to the latest and only Loan Executives hired by IXL Bank.

The first customer entered Garrett's office and settled comfortably in the wooden chair. Surprisingly enough, she failed to comment on the ugly and unprofessional setup of the office and this indicated that she was probably from the lower and slummier section of the city.

'So what can I do for you today?' asked Garrett in a helpful tone.

'I need a big loan; a really big loan.' The woman's voice was husky like that of a chain smoker.

'I'll need to hear your name and see paper's for collateral, ma'am.' Garrett was absolutely sure that this woman was planning to run with the money.

She reached into her over-sized and shabby handbag and drew out a collection of ruffled and crumpled files. She put them on the table and with a sharp eye movement indicated for Joe to look them over.

Joe pulled the sheets towards him and started glancing over them slowly.

Driver's licence: Fake. Voter ID card: Fake. Car registration: Fake. Home owner papers: Fake.

'Everything looks good....Miss Ruby Diamond,' murmured Joe. Lying wasn't his forte and he did his best to maintain a straight face.

Ruby Diamond was by far the stupidest fake name Joseph Garrett had ever heard.

'Thank you sir,' replied Ruby Diamond and then just sat there looking at the wall.

A few minutes passed and Garrett decided to ask the obvious question and break the silence.

'What kind of loan are you looking for Miss?'

The woman looked around hopelessly and retorted weakly, 'What kind of loans are there?'

Garrett attempted to maintain his composure in the ridiculous situation. 'There are personal loans, business loans, car loans, home loans, education loans.'

Ruby Diamond replied quickly, 'I want a personal loan. That's what I want, a personal loan.'

She was clearly a horrible liar.

'And the value of this loan would be?' prompted Garrett.

'Wait! I get to choose how much money I get?' asked Ruby Diamond foolishly.

'Well, if you have the collateral to back it up. Sure.' Joe was annoyed beyond recognition.

'Okay, I want 2,000. No, 20,000. No, 200,000.' Ruby Diamond grinned ecstatically at the thought of all that money.

'Alright then,' murmured Garrett simply hoping to imagine what this woman will be able to accomplish with all that cash.

Joe pulled the piece of paper labeled 'Loan Application' close to him and took a deep breath. He then stamped a big red 'Approved' onto it and watched the woman he knew as Ruby Diamond, snatch up the paper and dance out of the room, leaving everything else behind. This was ridiculous.

That same evening, the three Loan Execs of IXL Bank headed to Jimmy's house to sit down and discuss numbers. Upon entering the little three bedroom home, the three men headed upstairs and comfortably settled in the living room.

Jimmy's house was more like the home of a man named James Wolfenstein than Jimmy. The entrance was protected by a menacing black gate while the boundary of his property was fenced by an electrified barb-wire and fifteen foot high towering walls. The two-storeyed house, surprisingly, only had three bedrooms and was the only home in the neighborhood to have slanted snow-roofs. The walls of the home, on the outside, were painted a dark purple and the inside was layered with pitch-black carpeting and silver walls. Paintings hung in great numbers and most of the furniture was more classic than contemporary. This, however, directly conflicted with the fact that the home of James Wolfenstein had a top-notch electronic home security system with cameras that were connected to a cloud server for remote access. Even his laptop and cell-phone were the best money could buy and entire rooms had been converted for his work with accounts and computers. His private work room had a four-monitor display with dual CPUs and handwritten notes plastered from wall to wall. This truly was the home of a well-cultured whiz-kid.

Dime and Garrett rested on the suede sofas as Jimmy brought out a six pack of international beer from his fridge and placed it on the table. Both guests greedily reached out and popped them open with nothing but their thumbs.

'Does anybody want ice?' asked Jimmy tiredly as he stood next to the fridge.

Both men declined,shaking their heads, and Jimmy settled down next to them, popping open the third beer of the pack for himself.

'So let's run numbers boys,' said Jimmy as both Dime and Garrett grunted from post-work laziness.

'Oh come on Jimmy, we'll talk figures later. The big baseball game's on tonight.' Dime was trying to be persuasive, but Jimmy was too much of a dedicated worker to be persuaded by fantasies of fun-filled evenings of watching national-level sports with friends.

'Let's just do this so we can get on with relaxing without having to worry after that?' said Jimmy as he once again attempted to reason with his fellow colleagues.

'Alright fine,' said Dime reluctantly as Jimmy passed around sheets of papers and pens.

The next thirty minutes were spent in silence as all three men ran numbers relating to the loans they had given out that day. It wasn't an easy task as each figure had been recorded in memory and some were over seven digits long. This was one of the reasons that Jimmy had wanted to get everything on paper as soon as possible. The numbers might not have been as accurate if the work had been done after relaxing for a couple of hours.

Garrett was the last one to finish and breathed a sigh of relief when he was done.

'So who's going first?' asked Dime as he sipped his beer.

'I'll go,' announced Jimmy and continued in monotone, 'Four loans of value dollars one million seven thousand.'

'I'll beat that,' butted in Garrett and went on to announce his damage for the day, 'Three loans of value dollars two million four hundred and seventy three thousand.'

Jimmy put down his beer and clapped in respect and appreciation.

Dime remained quiet and looked at his friends nervously.

'Come on Dime, give us your numbers,' said Garrett in bloated competitive spirit.

Dime took a deep breath and said, 'Two loans of value dollars one hundred and twenty one thousand.'

The friendly competitive mood dropped and was quickly replaced with a grim ambience.

'You really got to pick it up from tomorrow. You got that Dime?' Jimmy spoke as a friend giving helpful advice.

Jimmy then turned to Garrett and asked, 'What's the total?'

'Three million six hundred and one thousand,' replied Garrett with a wide grin on his face.

The downfall of IXL had begun.

Castles Made of Sand

Twenty-seven days had passed since the three men had infiltrated the ranks of IXL. Things had gone pretty smooth as the higher level management had been swamped with cartons of paperwork and wining and dining big clients. This had allowed Jimmy, Garrett and Dime to get on with their espionage easily and there was no doubt that they had been more than successful.

Mulligan's car waited in front a small white gate as the lazy guard leaned out of his booth and hit a little black button. The electronically operated gate, as most gates were now days, swung open with gradual momentum and the pitch black Cadillac Sixteen rolled through.

Mulligan sat dressed in appropriate golf attire as his car entered the exclusive Alligator International Golf Club. A very absurd name, as Mulligan had first noticed, because there were no alligators for at least five hundred miles, in any direction. The name, however, was well known in rich communities and after the success of the club here, many other branches had popped up in different cities.

The car drove past the parking lot on the immediate left, which was seemingly packed with some of the most expensive vehicles in the world and then across a large grand looking clubhouse, which served as a home to a variety of restaurants, but mainly operated as a small seven-star hotel.

The car finally pulled up and Mulligan got out. A small electrical golf cart sat waiting for him and several employees, who Mulligan had tipped massively on previous occasions, greeted him with extensively wide grins. His golf set was quickly removed from the boot of his Cadillac by his driver and then safely fastened on to the back of the golf cart. Mulligan quickly got behind the wheel of the tiny vehicle and zoomed past those who had hoped to gain unnecessarily large tips and headed towards the tee-off of the 'A' course.

The massive Alligator International Golf Club had a sprawling 54 holes divided into three courses, designated 'A', 'B' and 'C'. As with most other clubs, these categorizations were based on the difficulty of a set of 18 holes with 'A' being the hardest and 'C' being the easiest. Aside from that, this private golf community had one of the highest rated hotels in the city and was known for its notoriously strict membership laws. Mulligan had, fortunately, received the benefit of transferred membership from his father and had now earned the luxury of using the course as and when he pleased.

The impressive golf course had one of the most magnificent designs and was rated the eighth best course in the world. Using all of this to his advantage, Mulligan had used the funds of the Royal Citizen's Bank to purchase two golf carts, which he often used when hoping to woo important clients or to impress his seniors from the upper management.

Mulligan stepped down on the soft accelerator of the golf cart and felt the speed increase. He then navigated through the complicated pathways of the course, without a map, and minutes later, arrived at the little open-air shed that served as the check-in counter, before the first hole. Upon arrival, he saw that Jimmy, Dime and Garrett were already there and judging from the lack of sweat, he realized they had only been there a few moments.

'Boss, they're saying that there's a four and a half hour wait. Apparently, two four balls of gold members just arrived so we're going to have to go after them,' informed Jimmy apologetically.

'Don't worry about it guys,' said Mulligan with the tone of a man who knew what he was doing. He approached a gruff old man, sitting behind the counter with a register in his hand. It was his job to keep account of whoever played on the course.

The man who was dressed in a frail blue half-sleeved shirt and khaki shorts looked at Mulligan questioningly.

'We're going to tee-off now,' said Mulligan with a wave of authority.

'I just told your friends there son, you can't...' The old man's sentence ended too soon as Mulligan flashed a titanium 'Platinum Privileges' card with his name inscribed at the bottom.

A quick adjustment was made in the register and the old man weakly indicated for Mulligan's party to go on ahead.

Mulligan, Jimmy, Dime and Garrett stepped onto the tee of the first hole with their clubs in hand and their eyes on the pin. Mulligan's ongoing mental assessment of the hole, however, was quickly interrupted as a twenty-five-year-old bratty-looking kid barked in his ear, 'Get out of here old man. We're going first. We're gold members.' The brat was clearly proud of the golden card that he was sticking in Mulligan's face.

The loud-mouth, however, quickly backed off as Mulligan gently shoved him away with the head of his five-iron and flashed the same all-powerful card that he had shown the old man, just a few moments earlier. Intimidated by the power that the titanium platinum card held in front of him, the brat retreated from the tee and let Mulligan get on with his game.

Even though a nice friendly game would have been enjoyed by everyone, the purpose of this golf game was for Mulligan to receive a final update on the IXL endeavour as preparations were to be made. The decision as to whether the branch would remain open or be sold off would be taken in a mere three days and Mulligan needed to be prepared for every possible outcome. Mulligan's meeting with three employees of a rival bank would clearly raise some flags and, therefore, this had to be done discreetly. Sure, the three men could have met in a private board room or at one of their houses, but then Mulligan would have missed his weekly golf game. This seemed to be the only way to kill two birds with one stone.

By the third hole, Mulligan was at scratch with the other three, at least a couple of strokes over. Dime and Garrett were clearly in awe of their boss because of his impressive golf handicap and high position at the club, but Jimmy, on the other hand, had remained indifferent as he was now used to his boss doing impressive things all the time.

Jimmy had a theory about his boss, and given that all he knew, it seemed to fit. The lack of family and minimal personal social life had given Mulligan the time to cultivate and perfect himself in almost every way. This allowed him to shine at business gatherings and impress people easily. His was the ultimate sacrifice of home life for work life and Jimmy doubted as to if it was worth it.

Cigarette in hand, Mulligan strolled towards his ball, lying fifty yards ahead, and thought about how great a sport golf was. He relished the verdant soft grass of the fairway, the elegance of the green, the magnificence of the strategically placed water bodies and sand traps. His experience was further complemented by the perfectly hot 35 degrees Celsius temperature and 12mph breeze that carried the friendly chirping of the sweet birds that hovered above.

Nearing the end of the twelfth hole; Dime, Garrett and Jimmy had conveyed every last detail of their work at IXL to Mulligan. It was important that he knew everything so then he could sort out all the relevant information and focus on it. He could have, of course, asked the three men to keep their reports short, but he wasn't sure that even they knew what relevant information to filter in and out.

At the end of the game, the four men sat in the club restaurant feasting on sandwiches and gulping down energy drinks. 'You've done well boys. I'll give you that. Much better than I expected, to be honest.'

Mulligan's uplifting words were appreciated by all.

'Thanks boss,' replied Dime with a wide grin as he continued to hog on his food.

'But there is one other thing,' said Mulligan solemnly.

The eating stopped and all three men listened with slight annoyance. They had done everything he had asked them to.

He couldn't possibly ask for anything more.

'To ensure that the board does, in fact, shut IXL down, they're going to need a little loss of faith.'

The men continued to listen and hope that their boss would clarify this riddle.

'The board will inevitably ask for Mr Hughes to appear before them tomorrow and I need you to make sure that he doesn't come. Do whatever you have to. We can't have that tired old alcoholic talking the board into giving him another chance.'

The three men nodded understandingly and realized that Mulligan was right. Now that they had come this far, it was best to ensure victory.

Mulligan left his employees alone to scheme and decided to head back to the office.

'So what do you think we should do?' asked Garrett breaking the thoughtful silence.

'Do we have him put down?' asked Dime innocently, but quickly decided to withdraw his suggestion after being flashed looks of disgust from his colleagues.

'We can't go that far. We can have him kidnapped though,' said Jimmy, attempting to picture what that would be like.

'No, that's still too illegal. If we attract too much attention like that, we can get into a lot of trouble.'

Garrett had been right and the other two men nodded as they realized the full weight of the situation.

'What if we have him killed and make it look like a mugging? Or a burglary?' asked Dime once again, hoping that the other two will go for his suggestion.

'There's too much that could go wrong,' said Garrett, attempting to make his fellow friend understand that they could not kill the man.

For the next few minutes, all three men remained lost in deep thought.

'Suicide?' suggested Dime, excitedly breaking the silence.

'We're not killing Ted Hughes! Do you understand that my friend?' barked Jimmy angrily.

Garrett quickly looked around and made sure that no one had heard their conversation while Dime slouched back into his chair with an annoyed look on his face.

'Here's what I think we should do.' Garrett spoke confidently. 'We put a sedative in his whiskey tomorrow so when he decides to take a little drink after lunch, he'll be out for the entire day and is going to end up sleeping through the board meeting. What do you think?'

'That could work,' answered Dime.

'Sounds good,' echoed Jimmy.

'So what sedative do you think we should use?' asked Garrett, determined to delve into the details of the plan.

'Leave that to me. I'll make sure that the sedative's in the bottle.' Dime had been a prankster as a teenager and was familiar with certain stealth techniques that might be required to finish this task.

Garrett was annoyed that he had been cut off from the implementation of his own plan and simply nodded in response.

Jimmy remained indifferent and simply hoped that everything would work out.

Two hours later, Dime sat in the driver's seat of his custom black Nissan GTR and sped down the road at nearly three times the speed limit. Many traffic cops had seen and recorded his speed, but none of them would bother to take on the risk and dangers of chasing down a buffed-up car at 250 kilometres per hour, down a semi-crowded road. It was reckless. Clearly Dime's taste in clothes also matched his exceptional taste in vehicles.

Dime had already placed a call to one of his contacts a while earlier, and was headed to a slum in the lower city to pick up the sedative he had asked for.

The loud and powerful sound of his engine attracted a great magnitude of attention from the teenagers who belonged to the poor local neighbourhoods. Dime proudly drove his flawless car past them and towards his destination. He knew he had given those who had seen his car something to brag about for days to come.

After rounding through a couple of filthy ill-kept streets, the GTR finally came to a halt and it's owner, clad in golf attire, got out and engaged the custom-built triple lock. Better to be safe than sorry. Dime then paced down a back alley and saw his contact waiting for him. Neither man knew the other's name for obvious reasons, but Dime was sure that his contact was richer than he looked. The man was wearing a navy-blue hoodie and baggy jeans. His ring-covered fingers held a brown package. His pale white face was concealed by oversized aviator sunglasses. Dime handed a roll of money to the man who quickly handed the package in return.

'How does this work?' asked Dime as the seller stood counting the cash.

'Drop it in whatever and, three seconds later, a single drop of it will put you to bed for a long time.'

Dime nodded and when he saw that the man had finished counting the cash and had approved the amount, he began to walk back to the car. As he once again retraced his path through the winding alley and saw that his car remained intact, just as he left it, he breathed a sigh of relief.

Theft ran rampant in the neighbourhood and he considered himself lucky for not having his vehicle stolen.

Dime got in and the car growled to life, once again drawing the looks of nearby men and children and giving them something to talk about. He hit the gas and the upgraded acceleration kicked in, causing his car to go much faster than it naturally would have. Minutes later, he was on the bridge, speeding to the safer side of the city.

Realizing his mistake in thinking of the other side as the 'safer' side of the city was something that he instantly mentally corrected. The metropolis was divided into two even halves and each half was as bad as the other. One half was home to a poverty stricken population who couldn't even afford the toll to cross the bridge to get to the other side of the city. Such levels of extreme poverty drove men and women to inhuman crimes, out of desperation, and even though the law enforcement presence was strong, there was only so much that the cops could do.

The other half of the city that was home to Park Woods, The Royal Citizen's Bank, Brookstone Bank and other such world-class establishments was equally bad as the poorer part of the city. One prevailed in blue-collar crimes while the other dominated white-collar felonies.

The next morning, Dime sat at his uncomfortable desk and remained as calm as ever. The fact that he had to drug his boss, within the next ten minutes, failed to make him even slightly nervous. Having safely tucked the 'magic' pill next to his cuff-link, all he had to do was get close enough to the whiskey to let the pill slip in unnoticed and then occupy his boss's attention as the pill dissolved for the next three seconds.

After formulating his game plan for the next few minutes, he decided to head down to the office of Ted Hughes. The secretary blushed as she watched Eugene Dime arriving, dressed in his latest beige suit and bright-white silk shirt. He had forgone wearing a tie today, and his top button hung open, revealing a bare chest that excited the charmed secretary.

'Do you have an appointment, Eugene?' asked the secretary as she blushed. It had only taken them a month to get to know each other on a first-name basis.

'Do I need one?' asked Dime suavely

The secretary blushed and buzzed her boss who asked for Dime to be sent in.

'Go right in, Eugene.' The secretary clearly liked using his first name as much as she could and even though he was not used to being called anything but 'Dime,' he had developed a liking for it.

Winking at the secretary as he walked by, Dime strolled into his target's office and returned to focusing on the matter at hand.

Not surprisingly, the symbolic whiskey bottle lay on the oak desk and as Hughes had developed a friendly relationship with Dime over the past few weeks, he had stopped hiding his addiction for alcohol from his trusted employee.

'So, what's going on Dime?' asked Hughes as the man he was talking to took a seat across him.

Sticking with his pre-planned story, Dime got to work. 'I'm really stressed boss. I might not have a job after today. I've heard the board is probably going to shut us down.'

Hughes empathized with the fake sadness and as Dime had predicted, he inevitably said, 'Do you want some whiskey?'

Barely managing to keep his act up after the almost instant accomplishment of his task, Dime spoke grimly, 'Yeah, definitely boss. Do you think I could have a glass though?'

Hughes nodded and instead of buzzing his secretary as Dime thought he would, the man got up and walked to a cabinet on his left. This made things much easier. During these precious few moments, Dime let loose the pill from under his cuff-link and dropped it in the bottle. Luckily, the three seconds needed to dissolve had easily passed and Hughes had not seen a thing as he pulled out glasses from the metallic looking shelf inside the cabinet.

Now focusing on getting out of the room, Dime pulled out his cellphone and put it to his ear in order to fake a phone call. 'Good morning sir. How are you today?' asked Dime as the fake call began.

Hughes quickly turned and saw that his employee was on the phone. 'Call him back later. You need to relax right now,' he said, as he attempted to woo Dime into staying.

Dime, however, quickly got up and started walking to the door with his phone to his ear and softly nodding as though he was listening to instructions. He then put his hand on the bottom end of the phone, so that the non-existent customer wouldn't hear, and softly responded to his boss, 'sir, I really need to go. This is a big client. I'll come back later.'

Then, without waiting for his boss's response, Dime escaped the room.

That same evening, the three traitors of IXL Bank headed to Mulligan's estate to watch the result of the board meeting on the news.

The greatness of the home had never failed to impress anyone and these three men were no different.

The four men sat across a hundred-inch projector screen and patiently listened for information as to whether their ploy had succeeded or not.

After sitting through a feature on domestic violence, the news they were awaiting finally came.

'The IXL Group has just finished with their board meeting and as many people have patiently awaited the fate of the bank, the decision has finally come. Due to an absolute halt in cash flow, bad administration and reputation-damaging customer care, the board has concluded that this branch of the IXL will be shut down.'

The four men burst into cheers and Mulligan even handed Garrett a champagne bottle to pop open. Their focus on the alcohol, however, was short-lived as the news report continued and took an interesting turn.

'The three biggest clients of IXL Bank are now without administrative and financial support and it is clear that The Royal Citizen's Bank and Brookstone Bank will clearly step in to pick up the spoils. The farmer's initiative, which was the largest account that IXL had handled, has announced that they hope to maintain their wealth, within the city, and that either Brookstone Bank or IXL Bank will be able to cater to their needs of personal care and privacy.

Thornton Plumbing and Nakamura Motors, the other two big accounts that IXL lost are also hoping to be catered with reliable service. At this cornerstone of financial instability within the city's economic structure, our analysts say that whichever bank gains the majority of the wealth that IXL has lost, that bank will gain a powerful advantage over the other.'

The mood suddenly dropped as the four men realized that the destruction of one potentially formidable enemy had inadvertently thrust them into a war with another.

Thirty minutes after the ending of that report, the other three men left and Mulligan went back to enjoying his solitude. The news report, however, had left him in a sour mood and he knew it was best to go out and enjoy himself rather than to keep thinking about it and get frustrated.

Dressed in his classiest black suit with a black shirt, Mulligan decided to add a black fedora to his attire today and it suited him brilliantly.

He left his home and gave his driver instructions to take him to Roger's; the only place in the city where every man's eccentric need could be satisfied.

After driving past the extravagant buildings of the upper city, the car finally skidded to a halt in front of an extremely dark alley. Mulligan got out of his car and walked towards the darkness. From countless experience, the man knew where he was going. A three-minute walk later, he arrived in front of a short staircase, leading downwards toward a green door, with two big bulky men standing next to it in overcoats.

Mulligan could only imagine the variety of weaponry they carried.

'When were you last here?' asked the guard to the left, in a deep voice.

'1968,' replied Mulligan.

Upon successfully answering the access question, one of the guards opened the door for him and Mulligan strolled into a different world.

Roger's was regarded as the epitome of the underworld. Anything was possible, once you set foot in the place. The walls were a bright white and the floor was covered with a big red furry carpet.

Roger himself was dressed in a white tuxedo and red shirt. He headed towards Mulligan, dancing along the way, matching the beat of the 1940s dance song playing through the speakers.

'Mr Mulligan!' he exclaimed, with pleasure in his French accent, and then leaned in to give his client a hug.

Mulligan returned the hug and was then escorted through the thick crowd of men and women towards a private booth in a secluded area.

Mulligan quickly took his place in the booth and Roger

introduced him to man while maintaining a massive grin, 'This is Emanuel. He's my number one man. You're a VIP here, Mr Mulligan so you just tell Emanuel whatever you need and he'll get it for you, booze, women, cigars or anything else. When you feel like putting some money down, Emanuel will take care of that too, okay?'

Mulligan nodded in response and upon seeing that his client was okay, Roger waved and walked away.

Besides all the glamour that filled the room to an intoxicating amount, Roger was pretty much a glorified bookie. He bet anything and everything. Mulligan was one of his oldest customers and had bet on everything from street races and college basketball games to the ending of movies and who the latest No.1 on the world music charts will be. Given that Roger was the bookie and Mulligan just a man treating himself, it was very rare that the outcome of almost any bet was not in the bookie's overall favour.

After lighting an illegal cigarette that Emanuel had brought him, Mulligan thought about what he wanted to bet on tonight. Even with the roaring laughter and music that filled his ears, he easily weighed the pros and cons of every bid and after about seven minutes of consideration, hailed Emanuel to his table.

'What are the odds on that big race, down in the purple district?' asked Mulligan coolly.

'One is to three with the GTR as the underdog,' replied Emanuel robotically.

Mulligan nodded and then withdrew a wad of cash from his pocket. From the thick roll of bills, he pulled out the sum he was looking for and handed it to Emanuel.

'I want ten grand on the GTR.'

The rest of the night flew by quickly as Mulligan treated

himself to everything and anything his heart and mind desired. Sadly though, even though as imaginative as a man Mulligan was, most of what he desired came in the form of exquisite tobacco and alcohol, in elegantly shaped bottles.

The next morning, Mulligan sat in his office smoking his first cigarette of the day. The comfort and raw sense of power he felt with a cigarette in his hand was something that no substitute could replicate. He had tried hard to quit, once upon a time, and like many others, had failed miserably.

As the smoke left his lungs, his elbow automatically reduced the angle and his hand brought the cigarette once again to his mouth. Thoughtlessly, he inhaled the fumes of doom and thanked God for allowing him to feel sensations as great as he was feeling now.

The phone buzzed and shattered his trance.

'What is it?' asked Mulligan impatiently.

'Jimmy's here. He wants to see you,' said his secretary softly.

'Send him in,' retorted Mulligan and contemplated as to whether or not to stub out his cigarette.

It easily had another two drags left in it.

The door opened and Jimmy walked in with a nervous look on his face.

'What's going on kid?' asked Mulligan with genuine concern; a truly rare emotion in his case.

'I've been thinking about it boss and it is critical for us to secure the majority of the leftover clients after the IXL debacle.'

Jimmy spoke much faster than normal.

'I know that kid. I'm already working on some strategies for the big players,' replied Mulligan hoping to implant confidence in the young man.

'I know boss, but I'm unsure as to whether some strategy will be enough.'

Mulligan let the insult pass. The kid was too stressed out to realize what he was saying.

'Brookstone is planning to bring in some smooth-talkers and I think we should do that too.'

Mulligan nodded. He had come to a relatively similar conclusion and already had someone in mind.

'I'll take care of it, Jimmy. I want you to take the day off and relax. Hit the beach or something.'

The kid nodded and slowly walked out of the room. The anxiety was getting to him.

Mulligan resumed his chain-smoking and simultaneously buzzed his secretary.

'Yes boss?' she asked robotically.

'Set up a call with the Chairman.'

The Chairman was the man who sat at the very top of the ladder. He pulled every string there was to pull and held on to a dangerously large amount of power. People feared him as much as they respected him and Mulligan was no different. This wasn't a man who was free to talk at any time of the day. Call requests were screened and prioritized based on who the caller was and what the topic of conversation would be.

The Chairman, however, was also a man who valued his top people and Mulligan was one of them. So when he was informed that the regional bank manager wanted to talk to him, the Chairman had bumped the call up to a mere four hours away. Even though it sounded like a relatively large amount of time, people who knew and understood the potential of the being that was the Chairman realized that four hours was a grand privilege. Most people had to wait days, some even weeks; all for a couple of minutes of conversation time.

The time finally came and Mulligan's nervous foot-tapping finally stopped. He stubbed out his cigarette, cleared his throat and then answered the call.

'Mr Mulligan. How are things?' inquired the Chairman's elegant voice.

'Things are…unpredictable, sir.' Mulligan had chosen his words carefully.

A moment passed.

'And where does this unpredictability originate from?'

'We're about to engage in a struggle for clients and have no absolute way of ensuring victory.'

'Absolution is a rare thing.'

'Even so, I would like to have at least some sort of advantage.'

'Are these clients the remnants left in the wake of your demolishing IXL?'

'How…how did you know sir?'

'I have my sources.'

'Clearly.'

'So what do you need? Funding?'

'Not exactly, I'm actually looking for a talent of some sort.'

'Define talent.'

'Someone who has the ability, facial correctness and charm to lure and woo customers into our favour, someone who can adapt his approach, based on the kind of person he meets.'

'These are extremely specific demands.'

'Yes, I am aware of that sir.'

'Shouldn't you be talking to Human Resources, if you want to hire someone?'

'Actually sir, I believe the person I am looking for is already under contract with us, sir.'

'You've clearly done your research, Mr Mulligan.'

'Yes, I have. It is important to be precise. Things get done more efficiently.'

'Didn't we offer you a job at the Head Office yet?'

'I was offered a promotion, sir. I respectfully declined.'

'Why?'

'I work better down here.'

'Fair enough, so who do you want?'

'Someone I recruited for the Head Office, a few years ago. His name is Caesar.'

Strange Days

Four Years Ago

A newly purchased Cadillac Sixteen roared through the streets, and the driver watched the cars in front of him scurry to the sides, as though an ambulance was passing.

A firm grip on the steering wheel and an acute control of the accelerator allowed the driver to employ a classic Japanese street-racing skill, and drift through the corners, while losing only a negligible amount of speed.

The driver saw a gridlock ahead and quickly jammed the breaks. The car slowed down to a smooth halt and a little grin that appeared on the driver's mouth was a sign of the fact that he was happy with his most recent vehicular purchase.

Another twenty minutes of driving time later, the car arrived at its destination and Mulligan parked outside the gate of a large and impressive mansion. He got out wearing a black overcoat and black fedora that protected his suit and leather shoes from the heavy rain that fell from the dark sky above.

He strolled over an intensely wet sidewalk where almost every second step of his would land in a puddle and further ruin his black leather shoes. He finally arrived at the gate and two burly security guards approached him. The one to his right frisked him, top to bottom, and upon finding a Smith & Wesson Model 625 tucked into his overcoat, he asked coldly,

'You can have this back when you leave, Mr Mulligan.'

The guard then took the gun away, and placed it in his guardhouse, while the other guard led him towards a golf cart, parked on the right. Mulligan then, contrary to usual decorum, got in beside the guard instead of the seat behind him and calmly enjoyed the view of the desolate mansion in these harsh weather conditions.

The four-minute cart ride allowed Mulligan to take in the mansion as a whole. The main structure stood towards the back end of the plot while the rest of the area was simply a large vacant space of well-cultivated greenery.

A small fountain rested in the middle, which Mulligan noticed to be overflowing because of the heavy rain. The trees in the distance looked like oak, but Mulligan couldn't be sure as it was a pitch-black moonless night.

The cart finally pulled up in front of the main door to enter the mansion and Mulligan took in his gloomy surroundings for one last time before getting out.

The cart then sped away and Mulligan approached the door. His eyes searched for a bell of some sort, but it turned out to be unnecessary as a woman, dressed in uniform, opened the door and greeted him with a smile.

Mulligan studied her silently as he entered the mansion and finally escaped the rain. He arrived at the conclusion that she must be the offspring of a family who had been running and managing the mansion since it had been built. These things were quite common in cases of excessively grand structures such as this one.

'May I take your coat and hat, sir?' asked the woman politely.

Mulligan gave her what she asked for even though he

realized that she was more concerned about not dirtying the wooden flooring than his comfort. After placing the clothing on a nearby table, the woman led Mulligan through the mysteriously designed passages of the house. This mansion was no different from any other; almost every inch of the house had some form of wooden flooring. The walls were also mostly wooden, but of a much darker shade, and paintings hung on the walls of the corridors and most of the rooms. Marble statuettes were also placed almost everywhere and clearly whoever had decorated this house had more money than they knew what to do with.

The woman was indifferent to Mulligan's reactions to the awesomeness of the grandeur of the mansion and this implied that she must have seen this countless times before and had become familiar with it.

The duo finally reached a study where a man sat behind an extensively humongous desk, which was littered with unorganized paperwork from one end to the other. The man was whom Mulligan had taken this trip to meet and clearly was what Mulligan had expected.

The woman simply announced, 'This is Mr Mulligan' to her boss before automatically leaving the room.

The man who sat across Mulligan was a thirty-one-year-old, dressed in a black silk robe and leather slippers. His attire implied that he had no reason to respect Mulligan and, therefore, he made no effort to attempt to impress him. He made a sharp hand gesture, which indicated for Mulligan to sit down, and Mulligan did so.

'Good to have you here, Mr Mulligan. Thank you for coming all this way.'

'No problem at all, Mr Olyphant. This is only a small

gesture to show that we have high hopes of doing business with you.'

'You know, The Royal Citizen's Bank is the fourth bank to approach me in the last two days.'

'Well sir, the inheritance you gained from your uncle is a rather large amount and we only hope to protect it.'

The conversation was quickly interrupted, however, as a howling woman burst into the room and shattered the formal ambience. Her face was covered with tears and she had a black eye. Mulligan quickly realized that this was Marcus Olyphant's wife and he had been beating her.

'Look at this! Look at this! You've killed our baby!' she screamed as she lifted her top and revealed gruesome wounds on her belly, which had probably been caused by a belt. Mulligan's face was overcome with horror as he sat their frozen, unable to figure out how to react.

'Get out of here! I'm with someone I need to talk to,' screamed Olyphant back at his wife.

'I didn't even do anything wrong! You're just evil!' howled back the wife as her tears started to pour faster.

The situation was quickly resolved, however, as two women appeared and quickly grabbed the wife. One stuck a needle into her neck and Mulligan could only hope that it was a sedative.

Olyphant rubbed his nose with his hand as if he was trying to figure out what to say next and Mulligan's horror was amplified as he saw that Olyphant wasn't feeling guilt, but instead embarrassment. People like this were sadists of the highest order and often preyed on the opposite sex, without any reason or emotion. They simply had a need to make others feel pain.

Mulligan realized this and decided on an unholy course of action.

'I know what you are, Mr Olyphant.'

The other man looked up curiously and asked, 'What do you mean?'

'I know what you enjoy because I'm just like you. I, however, have found a way to keep my needs away from those close to me. If you want, I can take you to a sanctuary for people like us.'

'I would like that.'

'Alright, I'll head down and wait in my car. You should go put on a suit and meet me there.'

Olyphant exited his chair and nodded.

Mulligan was not happy with what he was doing.

As he waited in his car with rain gashing down from every conceivable angle, Mulligan pulled out his cellphone and dialled for Roger. A few rings later, Roger picked up as he always did and answered with a calming and jolly voice, 'Mr Mulligan! What can I do for you today?'

Mulligan took a deep breath and uttered the words that he would regret for the rest of his life, 'I need you to arrange for a woman at the Great Marina Hotel. She's going to be dealt with roughly so make sure she's open to that. I'm willing to pay a lot of money for this.'

Even though the request was highly illegal and unorthodox, Roger never turned down a request from a client who ended his sentence with 'I'm willing to pay a lot of money'.

After outlining a rough plan on how to meet this request, Roger replied coolly, 'It'll be done, sir.'

Mulligan let out a smile of relief and replied, 'Make sure you're there yourself. This isn't for me so I would rather have it that you and the client arrange this directly after today.'

'Okay, sir. I'll text you the room number as soon as I can.'

Just after Mulligan ended the call and slid his phone into his pocket, he watched as Marcus Olyphant arrived in the cart and then got into the car. The Cadillac Sixteen growled to life and slowly began to pick up speed as its driver hit the almost-empty four-lane road.

The two men sat in silence, but a slight smirk was continuously present on Olyphant's face. Mulligan hoped that the man was simply smiling because he liked the car, but deep down he knew that the truth was much more horrific.

Fortunately for Mulligan, the hotel was only a ten-minute drive away and the awkwardness disappeared as the car pulled into the grand porch and the keys were handed to a sharp-looking valet.

The valet let out an excited grin as he got into the mysterious and elegant Cadillac and Mulligan simply hoped that the man would park properly and not wreck the car by getting carried away.

Still in absolute silence, the two men strolled through the lobby and towards the receptionist. As they walked, Mulligan flipped open his phone and a text message from Roger read, 'Room 0047'.

The receptionist greeted them with a wide smile, but on the inside she simply perceived the two men as shady characters, wearing long and wet overcoats. 'My name is William Mulligan. I believe you have a key for Room 0047 for me.'

'I'll need an ID.'

Mulligan obliged her with his driver's licence and after obtaining the key, the two men were on their way to the fateful room.

Olyphant maintained an odd expression on his face. It was almost as though he was both anxious and paranoid, but the odd lighting meant that Mulligan couldn't be sure.

They arrived at the door and Mulligan slipped the magnetic key card in. A green light blinked on top of the handle and the door swung open. Upon entering, Olyphant and Mulligan were greeted by a woman in an exotic red dress, sitting on the bed, and Roger, dressed in a navy blue suit, standing beside her.

Upon seeing the woman, the first thing Mulligan did was look at Olyphant's face and notice the change in expression. Seeing his prey had excited the man and his face was now flushed in red.

'My work here is done gentlemen. It would be best if you dealt with each other directly from now on. Mr Olyphant, I hope I'll see you at my office sometime this week.'

Without waiting for a response, Mulligan exited the room and felt a growing sting in the back of his head. It was something that he rarely felt, but was intensely familiar with. It was his conscience nagging him to go back into the room, draw out the Model 625 revolver he had recovered from the guards at the manor and then put six bullets in Marcus Olyphant's face.

The woman in the red dress had a wide smile on her face. She was thirty-five at best and was probably doing this so that her child could attend college. No one deserved what was about to happen to her, but at least she was ready for it. Or was she? Could Roger have omitted some details about what was about to happen? It was highly possible. There was some relief in Mulligan's mind, however. At least the innocent Mrs Olyphant wouldn't have to suffer anymore. The vividness of her wounds probably meant that she was beaten on a daily basis and Mulligan was almost glad that he had put a stop to that. Was the horrible and tragic affair that he had just dived into truly worth it? Brookstone was clearly in the lead right now and maybe the dozens of millions of dollars that Olyphant was going to put in the Royal Citizen's Bank would be the only thing that would even give him a fighting chance.

These questions and doubts quickly took over Mulligan's mind as he walked back through the lobby, received the receptionist's questioning gaze and then waited for the valet to pull up his car in front of him.

A few minutes later, the car screeched into the hotel and drove up the ramp at an unnatural speed. The valet stopped the car and got out with a wide grin.

Mulligan's face tightened and he barked at the valet as though he was on the verge of snapping, 'You ever take my car on a joyride again and I will sue you and this hotel for every last penny. You got that you little piece of garbage?'

The valet nodded his head in fear and then walked away. After watching the brat scurry, Mulligan entered his vehicle and drove into the darkness as agony and guilt engulfed his mind and heart.

A few days later, Mulligan sat in his office with a heavy heart. He still hadn't manage to push away the guilt of unleashing the monster that was Marcus Olyphant on the dozens of girls he was about to put in hospital for a long, long time.

Unpleasantly enough, the phone buzzed and Mulligan's secretary spoke with cold confidence, 'Jimmy and Mr Olyphant are waiting for you in CR:7.'

Solemnly, Mulligan got out of his chair and walked towards the chamber that held the greatest demon he had ever met.

He could only imagine the number of women he had already ruined for no rhyme or reason.

Upon entering, Mulligan saw that Jimmy was dressed in a white shirt, dark blue tie and beige pants. The fact that he wasn't wearing a coat seemed odd. On the other side of the room, however, Olyphant rested in a chair dressed in a plain black suit with a white shirt and no tie.

Jimmy, who was unaware of what his boss had done, started the conversation on a friendly note, 'I'm glad that you chose RCB as your bank Mr Olyphant. You will have the privilege of being a platinum client and we hope to take care of you in every way possible.'

Olyphant nodded approvingly and then turned towards Mulligan. 'Thank you for introducing me to your contact the other day. He's well connected and is good at what he does. I can see why you use him for yourself as well.'

Mulligan kept the horror that flowed through his blood within him and responded with only a slight nod. He couldn't even bear to look this man in the eye. Deciding to leave before he snapped and threw Marcus Olyphant out the window, Mulligan murmured, 'I'm feeling kind of ill so I think I'm going to head to the doctor's. Jimmy here is more than capable of handling your every need.'

Jimmy flashed a look of concern towards his boss, but then returned to his client with a wide reassuring grin.

Olyphant nodded indifferently and then Mulligan left the room. Even being in the same room as the man who attacked women for fun sickened him. He headed back to his office and lay down on the couch. His secretary was given strict orders to tell anyone, but Jimmy that he had gone home.

As he attempted but failed to take a nap, Mulligan seriously contemplated executing Marcus Olyphant. Killing him would be the easy and enjoyable part, but the problem was the aftermath. Since the contents of his will were not known, Mulligan knew that he couldn't risk Mrs Olyphant being left homeless, in case her husband had left everything to a nephew, mistress or charity. She had already been through hell and living in luxury was the best he could hope for her as her later years would draw closer.

As the end of the day came by, Mulligan heard a knock on the door, which was quickly followed by Jimmy entering the room.

'You okay boss?' he asked in a concerned tone.

'Yeah. I was lying about being ill.'

'I thought so. I just wanted to let you know that Mr Olyphant deposited 43 million. It's our biggest score yet. The Chairman's going to be happy. Actually now that I think about it, this is probably one of the biggest clients for RCB internationally.'

'43? That's actually more than I expected.'

'So boss, I'm going to go to the bar with Adam today to celebrate. You're more than welcome to join us. You look like you could use a night out.'

A celebration for signing a deal with a monster? It didn't sound too appetizing. Mulligan did, however, need for his spirits to be lifted.

'Yeah, why the hell not?'

'Alright!' exclaimed Jimmy and then continued, 'Meet us at SkyGlass at 8.00. It's on the roof of the Stinson building.'

Mulligan nodded in response and then watched Jimmy leave his office with an excited grin. He had no choice but to go now as he didn't want to disappoint one of his most reliable and trusted employees.

As promised, Mulligan's car pulled up in front of the Stinson building at 7.57 and then a three-minute walk through a desolate lobby and elevator ride up later, Mulligan sat at the open-air bar of SkyGlass at exactly 8.00 p.m., waiting for his employees to show up.

As Mulligan sat on his lonely barstool and observed his environment, it was quickly made clear to him that he was out of place. He had come dressed in a black suit with a pink shirt, but that clearly wasn't youthful enough for this place. SkyGlass seemed to be an extremely young and hip club with most of the customers being about half of Mulligan's age and dressed in extremely loud clothing.

Almost out of nowhere, the two familiar faces of Adam and Jimmy blended out of the crowd and approached Mulligan. They both greeted him with a smile and Adam murmured casually, 'It's good that you came. We'll make sure you have fun tonight.'

Jimmy nodded approvingly. Mulligan felt awkward and turned to the bartender who patiently awaited his order. 'I'd like vodka on the rocks.'

As Mulligan looked back at the two men, he was surprised to see them both suddenly smoking and upon looking around, it seemed that he was the only one who didn't have a cigarette in his hand.

Jimmy noticed his boss feeling out of place and offered graciously, 'Here, have a cigarette,' as he swayed to the loud upbeat music in the background.

'I've never smoked before,' murmured Mulligan in return.

'Just have a few. They're not addictive,' Adam repeated the greatest lie ever told.

Mulligan pulled out a cigarette from the box that Jimmy

held out for him and then lit it just the way he had seen it being done in movies a thousand times before. As the flame burned at the opposite end, he sucked on the filter and felt the lethal nicotine and tobacco enter his system for the first time. As with many first time smokers, the effect was awe inspiring. Hunger and stress washed further away with every drag. Only the beat of the music seduced his mind and a tide of epic calm took over his physical being. By the end of the night, the man was addicted.

The next Sunday morning, Mulligan followed his ritual of taking a long stroll through Park Woods, but this time he was accompanied by eighteen cigarettes and a double-gas lighter. He was dressed in a comfortable beige suit with a bright white shirt and black sunglasses. His cigarette further added a sense of danger to his already intimidating persona.

His stroll allowed him to soak in the sunlight and murmur pleasant greetings to his neighbours and other casual friends as he passed them by. He would even pet the occasional dog if it seemed cute enough to draw his attention.

His calm stroll was interrupted, however, as his phone rang. Upon drawing it from his pocket, however, he saw that it was an unknown number, but decided to answer it anyway.

'Who is it?' asked Mulligan gruffly.

'That's not important. I have a proposition for you. Meet me at the Roman Pillar in one hour. I have a feeling that you might want to hear this.' The reply was from an unknown man.

Even though Mulligan would have never agreed to something like this otherwise, there was an undeniable magnetism in the way the man spoke that was powerful enough to sway the strongest of wills.

'Fine,' replied Mulligan and then the call ended.

Maintaining his amazing punctuality, Mulligan arrived at the Roman Pillar exactly on time.

The maître d' recognized him as a regular customer and led him to a table that had already been reserved in his name.

The Roman Pillar was one of the top restaurants in town and had earned that commendation in every detail. From the paintings and décor to the cutlery and the way the food was presented, every single thing screamed pure Italian elegance. The food was of the highest quality and the tables were spaced out, just enough to provide a sense of privacy while maintaining the collective atmosphere of the restaurant. The carpet was of a dark green colour and the walls were painted a bright white. The ceiling was paved with a wooden design and the waiter's white and red uniforms complemented the entire design.

The maître d', on the other hand, was wearing a custom-made pitch black suit with a black bow tie. His sleekly parted hair and sharp eyes further showed his grooming, which matched the stature of divinity of the restaurant.

Mulligan was led to one of the best tables in the restaurant where a man dressed in a light blue suit and dark blue shirt awaited him. The man's hair was messy, but his features were chiselled and attractive. It was obvious, just by looking at him, that the magnetic voice on the phone had been his.

Slowly sliding into the chair across him, Mulligan studied the man with the utmost diligence. His stature was clearly of someone who was slightly over-confident and worked for himself.

'So who are you?' asked Mulligan coldly.

'Irrelevant. I wouldn't want to add weight to your mind by providing you with unnecessary information, Mr Mulligan.

I'm just here to offer you a proposition.' The strange man's voice was even more effective in person.

'So what's the deal?' asked Mulligan maintaining his cold tone and hoping for a less vague answer this time.

The man looked side to side as if to check for eavesdroppers and then leaned in closer. He spoke in a whispered and cool voice, 'I have been made aware that the Chairman of your bank is a man who appreciates fine art. Since it is almost impossible to get in touch with him myself, I was hoping that you could arrange a meeting between us.'

'Fine art? I appreciate it too,' lied Mulligan, 'What are you selling?'

'Selling is such a derogatory word. I am simply making some precious pieces of creativity and imagination available to those who understand and are willing to pay the monetary value of these fine artifacts.'

Mulligan was surprised by how well this mystery man could bend words. It truly didn't feel like he was selling anything anymore.

'So what paintings do you have?' asked Mulligan ignorantly. He was simply attempting to gain more information on this possibly fake product.

'I am not at liberty to disclose that information. I would have to answer that question directly to the Chairman.'

Mulligan nodded. He had spotted the first hole. This man was clearly working for himself and yet he was under a non-disclosure agreement. Something was fishy.

'Here's what we are going to do. First you're going to tell me your name.' Mulligan spoke aggressively.

'It's unnecessary,' replied the persistent mystery man.

A gun cocked under the table. Mulligan had withdrawn

his Model 625 revolver. It was no point attempting to out-talk this man. He was clearly much better at twisting words and bending truths than Mulligan would ever be, so instead, the decision to pull out a gun and act violent to intimidate the man had been made.

'Tell me your name or I'm going to blow out your intestines.'

Surprisingly, the mystery man maintained his cool under pressure. 'You can't shoot me in a crowded restaurant like this. It's too much of a risk and you know it.'

Mulligan forced his face to flush red and shuffled his eyes erratically. He knew how to act insane when he needed to. 'Do I look like I care about the risk? Now tell me your name.'

'Charles Woodstock.'

'Try again,' growled Mulligan as he easily saw through the badly implemented lie.

'Look, let's just enjoy our lunch in peace and then we can talk about this after.' The man's voice was amazingly smooth and it seemed to resonate with reason from beginning to end. Unfortunately, however, it failed to sway his opponent.

'Here's what we are going to do. On my count, both of us will get up and slowly walk towards the bathroom. It's towards the back. You try anything suspicious and I promise you that you will never walk again.'

The strange man realized that he had to do what Mulligan said and nodded in agreement.

Mulligan took a breath, put the gun back in his pocket, and then whispered calmly, 'Three. Two. One.'

Both men simultaneously rose from their seats and the man led the way to the restroom with Mulligan only a few inches behind him. The gun in Mulligan's pocket had been placed in such a way that he could shoot through his coat and still put a very painful bullet in the other man's spine.

The bathroom door swung open and both men entered. A quick look around from Mulligan ensured that they were the only ones there. He then locked the door behind him. The man who now realized that it was probably a mistake to have called Mulligan this morning, watched closely as the gun was drawn and he once again found himself looking down the thick barrel of the Model 625 revolver.

'So are you going to answer my questions or not?' asked Mulligan with unparalleled hostility.

'Yes I will,' replied the man. He could now only barely maintain his cool as he cowered on the floor with the cold steel of the hand-cannon touching his temple.

'Who are you and how did you get my number?'

'I'm just a businessman. I swear! I'm working for an art gallery!' The lie was convincing.

But Mulligan didn't buy it.

'Is it really that wise to lie with a gun to your head?'

Before the man could answer, there was a knock on the door.

Mulligan's attention shifted for a second and this mistake cost him as he felt a brutal punch land on his jaw. With the gun still in hand, Mulligan stumbled backwards while the man swiftly used the opportunity to return to his feet. Taking advantage of the situation, the man ran towards Mulligan who was already unbalanced and tackled him to the floor.

There was another knock on the door.

Mulligan, however, had managed to retain his structure by now and as the man lay on top of him, he grabbed him by the neck and stuck the gun into his gut. The other man struggled violently, but eventually managed to contain himself as he knew that the gun prevented any form of escape.

'Stay cool or I'll pull the trigger,' ordered Mulligan calmly.

'Open up! This is a public restaurant!' barked the Maître D's hostile voice from the other side of the door.

On Mulligan's queue, both men rose from the floor and slowly walked towards the door. The gun was constantly resting against the other man's hip to prevent any further struggle. The door was unlocked and the two men walked past the annoyed maître d' and out of the restaurant.

'Where are you taking me?' asked the man who was beginning to get sick of being at gunpoint.

'We're going for a walk,' replied Mulligan coolly.

Five silent minutes later, the two men strolled peacefully on the sidewalk as they headed towards an unknown direction.

'I've holstered my gun, but I would still like to have a peaceful chat,' said Mulligan softly as he broke the silence.

A few moments passed as a sense of relief flowed visibly through the other man and he replied honestly, 'I wasn't really selling any art. I'm actually just a scam artist. I don't see any point in further lying to you because clearly you can't be victimized and it's obvious that you won't go to the police either.'

Mulligan chuckled. He wasn't expecting such brutal honesty.

'So why are you still talking to me? Why didn't you bail the second I put away my gun?'

'I would have, but I feel that you have something interesting to say to me.'

'First, I want to know your name and how you got my phone number.'

'I go by Caesar. Your phone number's available to anyone

who offers to open an account with your bank. You might want to fix that.'

A smile grew on Mulligan's face. For some reason, he liked Caesar.

'Look Caesar, there's something about you that makes you magnetic. I don't know what it is, but what I do know is that it's very useful.'

'Why are you telling me this?'

'I want to hire you.'

'Why? I have only basic knowledge about how banking works.'

'That's irrelevant. You're going to be working for our Head Office to entertain and bring in some tough clients. Smooth-talkers like you are a rarity. Plus, you'll make more cash than you can count. So what do you say?'

Caesar let out a charming grin and replied suavely, 'Sounds like an offer I can't refuse.'

Smooth

As the plane rumbled, the pilot announced that bad weather had been causing the turbulence so there was nothing to worry about. Caesar wasn't much of a nervous flyer anyway so he ignored the thunderstorms that occurred just feet away from his window and continued to sip the delicious wine that the stewardess had provided him with the rest of his meal. First class was definitely the way to fly.

Being so close to the Chairman had often allowed Caesar to fly privately as well, but he knew that flying in your private plane was a dream that only a few men could bring to fruition. He took the last sip and then placed his glass down. He was glad that the flight was short because his need for a cigarette was beginning to kick in and he knew that no matter how hard he tried, smoking was something he couldn't resist.

After having disembarked and collected his baggage, Caesar walked out of the airport and quickly found Jimmy waiting for him. The kid had arrived in a Mercedes and was dressed in a black suit with a navy blue tie. Caesar, on the other hand, was dressed more comfortably in beige pants, a loose white shirt and black sunglasses.

'How you doing kid?' asked Caesar with his usual magnetic charm.

'I'm good sir. Can I take your bag?'

Caesar nodded kindly and the bag was quickly placed in the boot of the car. Unexpectedly, Caesar rode shotgun instead of sitting in the back like most of the other people that Jimmy picked up usually did.

The car revved to life and then Jimmy slowly proceeded to navigate through the busy airport road and onto the main street. As he took in his home city, Caesar lit a cigarette and felt bad that he hadn't returned here in the past four years.

'Sir, can I have one too?' asked Jimmy innocently.

Caesar granted his request and lit a cigarette for him. As the sun dropped down on the city below, the two men rode in silence with the sound of the engine pulsating in their ears and their lungs being filled by the beautifully toxic fumes of their cigarettes.

Halfway towards their destination, Caesar broke the silence and asked the question that was on everyone's mind. 'So what's the situation? The briefing I got at the Head Office was extremely vague.'

Jimmy structured his answer mentally, took another drag from his cigarette and replied calmly, 'Things are on edge. After IXL went down, a lot of clients were left unprotected and, therefore, we and Brookstone stepped in to pick up the pieces. The thing is, even though we had a greater market share earlier, this incoming flood of clients has perpetuated a war. Brookstone has been taking in every client they can find and we need to do the same if we want to maintain our lead.'

Caesar remained lost in thought for a few seconds and then posed another question, 'What about a sit-down for a fair division of clients?'

Jimmy chuckled, but not in a disrespectful way. Caesar realized that there was probably more to it than simple face value and his reasoning turned out to be correct when his question was answered, 'The media and the clients are too riled up to allow us to divide them up fairly. They demand attention and good treatment. Even Brookstone wouldn't be open to it as this would probably be their only chance to get ahead of us.'

'Damn it. It's never easy, is it?'

'Not around here, it isn't.'

'So where are we headed now? The office?'

'Yes. Boss wanted to meet you before you went to your hotel.'

'Where am I staying by the way?'

'We put you up in a suite at the Great Marina Hotel. You're our ace in the hole so we wanted you to be comfortable.'

'Alright.'

Caesar's cigarette ran out so he lit another one. The rest of the drive continued in silence as Caesar arranged the facts in his head. He silently hoped that his charm would be able to work as well as Mulligan hoped it would.

Caesar considered himself to be in the unending debt of Mulligan, as without him, he would still be running low-level scams instead of being on the verge of buying his own yacht.

Meanwhile, Mulligan sat smoking in the back seat of his Cadillac Sixteen as the driver continued to swerve through the endlessly dirty streets of the lower city. His mind was filled with an endless amount of thoughts and he had completely forgotten about the fact that Caesar was landing today and he had arranged for a meeting with him. Quickly deciding to fix his mistake, Mulligan flipped open his phone and called Jimmy.

Almost instantly, Jimmy answered with a curious voice, 'Jimmy here. What's going on boss?'

Mulligan took another drag of his cigarette and replied urgently, 'I'm headed downtown to meet Ponzarelli so I won't be able to make the meeting with Caesar. Take him to his hotel and tell him that I'll meet him tomorrow morning at the office.'

'Okay, sure boss.'

The call ended and Mulligan was grateful that he had Jimmy to rely on. The next few days were going to be intense and he needed people he could trust. Ponzarelli, on the other hand, wasn't someone Mulligan would grace with this hefty responsibility.

Donatello Ponzarelli was an old Italian Mafioso who ran almost all of the organized crime in the city. Unfortunately for Brookstone Bank and its manager Benjamin Dover, Mulligan had cultivated a special relationship with this man over a number of years, which would result in the Royal Citizen's Bank having a significant ally in this war.

The car pulled up in front of a seedy hotel named 'The Fisherman's Loft' and Mulligan got out. He dropped his cigarette to the floor and stubbed it out under his shoe. He pushed open the unguarded door and entered into a dark and gloomy lobby. Two unshaven men in cheap suits sat at the counter and Mulligan didn't need X-ray vision to know that they were carrying heavy firepower under their coats.

'Get out of here. This place is closed,' warned the man on the right.

'It's me. I need to see the Don.' The attitude of the two men behind the counter quickly changed as Mulligan stepped into the light and revealed his face.

'Place your guns on the table and head upstairs.'

Mulligan followed his orders and pulled out a pair of AMT Hardballer Long-slide pistols from his coat. Upon placing them on the table, he watched a hint of jealousy appear on the faces of the two guards as they admired the impressive pieces of hardware.

From what Mulligan knew about the black market, these two buffoons were probably stuck with simple Glocks. Even a Colt 1911 would be a big step up for them.

Another gangster dressed in a cheap suit entered the lobby. Since he was carrying a Remington shotgun, he was probably higher on the payroll than these two.

'I'm Santino. Come with me.'

Following instructions, Mulligan slowly followed Santino up a flight of steps and they then arrived onto a narrow floor, which was littered with countless mobsters. Dodging and excusing himself through the crowd, Mulligan continued to follow Santino as they headed up yet another flight of steps and onto a higher floor.

The second floor had a grand room across the staircase, which Mulligan had just climbed and four men guarded the entrance to the door.

'Wait here. The Don's already in a meeting. You can go in after he's finished.'

A nod in agreement assured Santino that Mulligan had understood the instructions and he began to wait patiently for the meeting to finish. The four men guarding the door eyed Mulligan repeatedly, but it was fruitless because he wasn't about to flinch.

Finally the door swung open and the mayor stumbled out of the room. He was carrying a briefcase in his hand and reeked of alcohol. As he headed towards the stairs, he muttered a weak, 'Hello Mr Mulligan' to which he received an astute, 'Good morning, Mr Mayor' in return.

It wasn't embarrassing to bump into people while waiting to meet the Don. Nearly everybody who was anybody had to deal with the Don sometime or the other. Failure to gain the Don's approval had been a weighing factor in IXL's downfall and was also one of the main reasons Benjamin Dover hadn't been able to get Brookstone's success to match that of the Royal Citizen's Bank. The Don's extensive influence was an asset that Mulligan treasured and protected with everything he had.

Mulligan entered the office and sat down across Don Ponzarelli. The war suddenly didn't seem that threatening anymore.

Don Ponzarelli was dressed in a custom black suit that had been stitched from the purest of fabrics. Under his coat, he wore a beautiful silk white shirt, which complemented his white hair. The man was about sixty-five years old, but looked about seventy-two. A life of violence and extensive alcoholism seemed to have that effect on people. His heavy face seemed even more dangerous because of a five-inch scar that ran across his nose.

'How are things?' asked the Don in a voice as smooth as olive oil.

'As you must know already, this war with Brookstone is taking its toll. I'm afraid we might lose our lead. Because of this, I must, with all my respect, ask you for help.'

'You have treated me well over the years and it is time for you to receive your reward. You have my full support. So now, tell me what exactly do you need? I believe a long vacation for Mr Dover will make all of your problems disappear.'

'I have kept aside that solution as a last resort. I would just like your blessing in case I decide to go through with it.'

'You have my blessing. Santino is available to you in case you need someone for the implementation.'

'Thank you.'

Mulligan rose from his chair and took a bow of respect. His first plan of action had been to implement a failsafe in case he couldn't win the war through conventional means and in this he had succeeded. In this city, the only way to get away with murder was with the help of the Don.

Back in his hotel room, Caesar studied the documents that Jimmy had given him. He wanted to identify the clients with the highest current and potential value so that he could prioritize them. The clients with the highest current value were the obvious ones, but to find the ones who would show immense growth in the next two to five years was the real trick.

After sifting through the paperwork for a while, Caesar remembered that he wasn't a conventional banker for a reason. He could get a good grasp on accounts, but something as detailed as predicting the chances of the success of a business seemed way out of his league. Pushing everything aside, he decided to focus on the real reason for his return to this city.

He opened a file, found the number he was looking for and then called. A few too many rings later, a smart voice answered.

'Farmer's Initiative. How can I help you?'

'Hi, I'm with the Royal Citizen's Bank and I was hoping to get a meeting with Mr Tim Rolan.'

'I'll put you through to his secretary.'

There was a short transfer beep, and then another efficient sounding secretary picked up.

'Mr Rolan's office. How can I help you?'

'I'm with the Royal Citizen's Bank. I need a meeting with your boss.'

'What about sir?'

'He'll know.'

'Okay. Can you make it in twenty minutes? Otherwise you'll have to wait until the day after tomorrow.'

'I'll be there.'

Caesar cut the call and let the phone drop on the bed. Within minutes, he was dressed in a black tie and suit with a perfected facial expression that inspired confidence. He then slipped out of his room and quickly headed down the lobby. Whether to drive himself or take a cab was a question that plagued him, but after realizing his stupid mistake of not asking for the address of the Farmer's Initiative building, he decided that a cab would be a better option.

He stepped out onto the porch and hailed a nearby valet. After being informed that there were no cabs in sight, Caesar decided that it would be best to simply take the hotel car and that's what he did. Fortunately enough, the hotel chauffeur knew where the Farmer's Initiative building was and in approximately nine minutes, he was there.

God bless the well-planned roads of the upper city.

Upon entering the building, Caesar was almost instantly confused by the architecture and simply finding the elevator took him a good four minutes. He glanced at his watch and realized that he was already a minute late. The elevator took him to the top floor, where he assumed the office of Tim Rolan must be. As soon as the monochrome silver elevator doors opened, however, Caesar quickly cursed himself for making biased assumptions as the top floor was simply a stock holding room. An unusual design decision, but one that was clearly effective if one thought about it. The floor was probably added after the building was made and therefore the top office floor would be exactly one down.

Caesar tapped the button and moments later he exhaled a sigh of relief as he entered the floor and found himself facing a large door that read 'Mr Rolan. Initiative Chancellor.' He knocked and then entered to find himself in a waiting room similar to that of Mulligan's.

The secretary greeted him with a smile and asked knowingly, 'Are you the gentleman from the bank?'

Nodding in acknowledgement, Caesar answered her question and was then given the go-ahead to enter the office. He pushed the brass door open and found himself in an office that was simple yet exquisite. White flourished everywhere and was scarcely contrasted by the prominently black furniture. Tim Rolan, a two-metre-tall muscular man, sat behind his grand desk and studied Caesar closely as he was greeted with a charming smile in return.

'Go ahead and take a seat,' said Rolan with an aura of command and leadership.

Caesar did as he was told and then extended his hand across the table for a handshake. Rolan shook the man's hand and then asked, 'So you're who exactly?'

'I'm Caesar. I represent the Royal Citizen's Bank.'

'I was wondering when I was going to hear from you guys. Brookstone's been hounding me ever since IXL went down and I wanted to hear other offers before I threw anyone a bone.'

'Well sir, the Royal Citizen's Bank assures you that your every need will be treated delicately and met with the most efficient response.'

'Good choice of words young man. Are you the Head of Regional Operations?'

'No sir, I'm a Client Prioritization Executive reporting from our Head Office. We want to make it clear that you are an important potential asset for us.'

'Look, it's clear that you know your way around words. But what I really want to know is, can you respond tactically in an urgent situation?'

'I assure you that we can sir.'

'Okay, answer me this then. Let's say, hypothetically of course, that I have an account in your regional branch. Six months from today, I find out that one of my protected farmers is facing land seizure for commercial use and I need to withdraw cash urgently to deal with permits and bribes or whatever. I call you on a Saturday night. What do you do?'

'We get you the money first thing Monday, of course. It would be lying in a briefcase before you even got out of bed in the morning.'

'That's not what I wanted to hear. I could go to any bank for first-thing-Monday service.'

'What else could we do?'

'You send me the cash after pulling it from your administration budget and then fill the gap first thing Monday when commercial account transfers begin to take place during business hours.'

'I'm not really sure if that's how things work with any bank.'

'Look, the Farmer's Initiative is one of the biggest institutions in the state. If you want our money, you better offer something more than Monday service.'

A moment passed as Caesar formulated a solution. He then pulled out his business card and passed it onto Rolan.

'That, Mr Rolan, is my personal number. This business card is not for commercial purposes as you can clearly see that it doesn't say RCB on it anywhere. You need something done urgently, all you have to do is put a call through to me and I promise you that I will have it taken care of within a couple of hours.'

'Now this is what I'm talking about. The best that fool Dover from Brookstone could come up with was an inter-link account scheme.'

'Well I'm glad I was able to get you to have faith in us. I hope you will give us the opportunity to treat you and this reputable organization in the most efficient and hospitable way we can.'

'You really do have a way with words son. And yes, I will give you our account.'

Both men got up and shook hands. Caesar smiled sharply and Rolan smiled back.

Minutes later, Caesar was back in the car being chauffeured back to the hotel. The ride was going to be much longer than usual because they had just hit rush hour. Since he wasn't doing anything anyway, he decided to call Mulligan to give him the good news.

A few rings later, his call was answered.

'Caesar, what's going on? I thought we had a meeting scheduled for tomorrow morning.'

'Yeah I know, but I decided to let you in on some good news. I just got out of a meeting with Mr Rolan and guess how it went?'

'You went to meet Tim Rolan without me? How could you be so irresponsible? Brookstone's been scooping clients already and I was relying on that account and a few others to maintain the lead.'

'Relax. Don't you think I can handle myself with clients? That's my job for god's sake. Well anyway, I got us the client.

He's going to come in one of these days to finalise the details.'

'You got lucky. I was pretty sure Rolan was going to be immune to your word-bending and charm.'

'Well he wasn't. I'll see you tomorrow.'

'Alri...'

The caller abruptly hung up. Caesar was clearly annoyed because of Mulligan's ungrateful reaction to the news.

The car continued to stand in gridlock and Caesar was quickly lost in thought. Scenarios of meeting with different clients plagued his mind and he wondered if he still had the ability to adjust and recover on the fly. Clients often made extremely unconventional demands and it was critical to make them feel safe by acting as though you had done something like that a thousand times before. His success with Rolan reassured him of his ability, but a seed of self-doubt still budded in his mind.

At the same time, Mulligan was back at the bank going over client information. He sat in one of the conference rooms as he didn't want to dirty his own office. In his hand, he held a file reading 'Farmer's Initiative' on the cover. As a cigarette leaned out from his mouth, the man considered the realistically probable size of the account and then compared it with what Brookstone was currently holding. With the way things were moving, there were only two or three other big clients that Mulligan needed to ensure that his bank would come out on top. While Dover had employed a strategy that involved him picking up any client that Brookstone Bank could get, Mulligan had made a tactical move to score the two or three big clients that pulled enough value to make sure that the Royal Citizen's Bank would not be left behind.

The next morning, Caesar sat in Mulligan's office dressed

in a beige suit and white shirt. To his left, Jimmy sat dressed in his usual navy-blue suit, across Mulligan who was comfortably resting in his leather chair with a plain black suit on. All three men had cigarettes in their mouths and Mulligan was reluctantly sharing his ashtray. On the table, between them lay two very powerful folders of information.

'I apologize for reacting badly on the phone yesterday. You did a great job scoring that account. It put us back in the dominant lead.' Mulligan spoke to Caesar with genuine emotion.

Jimmy, who hadn't yet heard the news, asked casually, 'What account? Must have been a big one if we're back in the lead. Brookstone had us on edge, otherwise.'

Mulligan answered the question, 'It's the Farmer's Initiative. Caesar went and spoke to Rolan himself yesterday.'

Jimmy led out a child-like grin and patted Caesar on the back. 'Great work sir!'

Caesar smiled his charming smile and nodded back a thank you.

'Okay, let's get down to business now,' said Mulligan as he brought in a more business-like mood.

'What's up?' asked Caesar as he took another drag from his cigarette.

'Even though we hit a big bonus with the Farmer's Initiative account, it's critical for us to go after a few other clients, otherwise Brookstone's going to speed past us and leave us drooling,' replied Mulligan coldly.

'Do you have any idea what kind of clients they'll have to get to come ahead of us boss? I think you're worrying for no reason,' said Jimmy in a relaxed voice.

'Look kid, Brookstone has big numbers. All the small-timers are being taken in by them. What we have to worry about is that if even one of those small-timers booms and becomes big, we're going to be done for. That's why we can't relax just yet,' Mulligan explained again in an icy tone.

Caesar considered the situation and agreed with his boss. Jimmy took another drag from his cigarette, but still remained unsure. His boss seemed to be getting paranoid.

'So who are our targets?' asked Caesar getting to the point.

Mulligan handed him the folders and began to explain the situation. 'There's about a dozen clients left uncollected right now, but only two of them are pertinent for us. The rest would probably swing towards Brookstone's playground even if we wasted time and energy on them. The first one is a Japanese car importing firm called Nakamura motors. They import cars from foreign districts and sell them here with a premium price tag. The only problem with this firm is that they don't have service centres for some of the brands so sales aren't always taking place in glorious numbers. I do believe that this company is going to show immense growth however, as local car producers are suffering from high labor costs and on the other hand, import tariffs and quotas are at an all-time low. The second one is a firm called Thornton Plumbing, headed by Phillip Thornton. The name probably makes what these guys do obvious and both of you are probably wondering as to why on earth I'd be interested in a local plumbing firm. The truth behind Thornton Plumbing, however, is that it's used by Don Ponzarelli to launder money and we all know that that kind of money is the best kind of money, especially in this city.'

Caesar took a drag from his cigarette. He then replied softly, 'I'll take Nakamura Motors. You should deal with

Thornton Plumbing because of your pre-existing relationship with the mob.'

'That makes sense,' replied Mulligan as he picked up the relevant folder while Caesar picked up the other.

'What should I do?' asked Jimmy as though he was feeling left out.

'Come with me. I might need you to address some questions that the client might have,' answered Caesar.

'Plus you'll see him show of his skills,' added Mulligan with a knowing smile.

Jimmy chuckled and then followed Caesar as he left the room. It was time to end this.

Caesar and Jimmy had been fortunate enough to be graced with the service of Mulligan's car and driver and they enjoyed being chauffeured around in a platinum black Cadillac Sixteen. Mulligan didn't plan on taking any action with Thornton Plumbing today and had instead decided to stay back at the office to do some research, leaving the other two men to pursue Nakamura Motors.

After taking a drive through an oak-tree filled area of the upper city, the car pulled up in front of a showroom near the harbour. Through the glass, Jimmy and Caesar saw a large variety of expensive foreign vehicles parked and ready to be sold. On the top of the structure, a white neon sign read 'Nakamura Premium Cars', which was probably impactful at night, but didn't attract much attention during the day.

Both men got out of the car and strolled across towards the entrance door, only to be greeted with a 'closed' sign and a dopey looking guard who was sleeping on duty. Upon hearing the two men loudly approach, the guard had woken up and barked 'We aren't open today!' which acted as a simple re-enforcement of the already prominent 'closed' sign.

'We're looking for the owner. Can you point out his office to us?' asked Jimmy coolly.

The guard studied the two men across him and then replied while still in a drowsy state, 'I don't know who the owner is, but the manager is off today. So if you want to find the manager, you can come back tomorrow and talk to him. Showroom hours are from ten in the morning to nine at night.'

'Thanks,' murmured Caesar in reply and then both he and Jimmy walked back to the car.

On the other side of the upper city, Mulligan found himself bored doing research in his office. He then made his usual decision of lighting another cigarette. The accounts of Thornton Plumbing had been cleaner than a hotel bathroom and without already having insider information, there was almost no way that Mulligan could have pegged the firm for being a front for money laundering. Don Ponzarelli was clearly good at what he did.

The phone buzzed and Mulligan picked up to hear his secretary's voice on the other end, 'sir, one of the tellers wants to talk to you. She has a complaint.'

Mulligan scoffed and replied, 'Tell her to man up and figure it out. If she can't deal with it in a week, then she can come speak to me.'

'Okay, sir. I will tell her, but she seemed upset. Anything else?'

'Yeah. I want you to call Phillip Thornton at Thornton Plumbing and ask him to come in for a meeting today. I want him here as soon as possible.'

'I'll get right on that.'

Mulligan put down the phone and hoped that he would

be able to get the Thornton Plumbing account by the end of the day. He knew he was being paranoid about losing the lead, but you could never be too careful in a war.

A few minutes later, the phone buzzed again and Mulligan picked up hoping to hear news about when Phillip Thornton would be coming in for a meeting.

'Mr Thornton is on his way. He'll be here in fifteen minutes,' informed his secretary.

As announced, Phillip Thornton arrived exactly fifteen minutes later and found himself sitting across Mulligan in CR:7. Thornton was a weak, frail looking fellow who was wearing a badly fitted suit and a loose hanging tie. Mulligan could clearly see why the Don had chosen him for a front as the man clearly had minimal to no will of his own.

'Mr Thornton, it was nice of you to respond so quickly. It spared me a lot of anxiety.'

'Well, I had a bland day so I decided to make the best use of it.'

'Okay, getting down to business, I would like to assure you that the fate of the Royal Citizen's Bank will not be the same as that of IXL. We are strongly grounded and have virtually no major difficulties.'

'Thank you for reassuring me.'

'So, what do you think about shifting your account to us Mr Thornton? We promise you the highest level of privacy and asset security.'

'I feel that Mr Ponzarelli wouldn't be happy if I went anywhere else and I had simply been waiting for your call. This just seems like a formality.'

'Well, that's perfect then. I'll ready up the paperwork and have it sent over.'

'That would be great. There is one other thing though.'

'What would that be?'

'Would it be okay if it was me who informed Mr Ponzarelli of this deal? I feel that it would make him happy and maybe help him forget about some mistakes that I've made over the past few months.'

'I understand.'

Both men then got up and shook hands. Thornton, for some unknown reason, maintained an apologetic expression and Mulligan wondered as to why this man had such low self-esteem. One thing, however, had become abundantly clear after this meeting: Don Donatello Ponzarelli had more influence and control than Mulligan had previously imagined.

One Night

Caesar rested calmly in the Great Marina Hotel swimming pool. The water was a little too warm for his liking, but he was still enjoying himself. A poolside waiter approached him and brought him the cranberry breezer he had asked for. Even though it was only eleven in the morning, he didn't feel guilty about having a breezer as he knew the alcohol in the drink was almost negligible for an everyday drinker.

Watching the other people in the pool, Caesar noticed that he was the only one who had come down here alone, almost everyone else was a part of a couple or family. Seeing fathers play with their daughters and mothers take care of their sons, Caesar wondered if he had made a mistake by giving up on the idea of a family.

His self-doubt soon passed as he looked down at his already finished breezer and then considered ordering another one. Looking at the large clock on the west wall of the hotel, he saw that he didn't have time and decided to get back up to his room. He tipped the waiter five dollars from his wallet and then dried himself thoroughly. He didn't want to get the carpeting inside the hotel wet. Even though nobody would say anything, Caesar had made a habit out of taking these sorts of precautions.

Back in his room, Caesar flicked on the television to

keep him company as he changed, and he noticed that all the news channels were raving on about the details of some new pandemic that had struck the city. Caesar ignored the trivialized piece of news and took a short shower. He then got dressed in a grey suit and white shirt while donning his latest black aviator sunglasses.

Dressed confidently, he returned to the elevator and headed down to the lobby. He checked his wristwatch to ensure that he was on time and observed his leather black shoes. They seemed to be getting old and Caesar knew he had to buy a new pair as soon as he could.

The elevator doors opened and he stepped out into the lobby. Jimmy, who was loitering around waiting for him, let out a smile as he saw the other man and they both approached each other and shook hands.

'Looking fresh, sir,' said Jimmy kindly.

'Yeah, I just got out of a swim. Did you get a car or should we rent the hotel one?'

'No need for that. I got a Mercedes from the office.'

Caesar nodded in approval and then both men stepped out onto the porch. Jimmy signalled to the waiting driver who quickly ran back to where he had parked and returned in a white Mercedes S-550.

'Hey you know, I drive a Mercedes too,' said Caesar proudly.

'Oh really?' asked Jimmy excitedly, 'Which one?'

'It's a sports; the Mercedes SLS.'

'That's impressive.'

'What about you kid?'

'I want to get the Lexus LFA Roadster when I can buy it, but I'm driving a Chevrolet Camaro right now.'

'Does it have stripes?'

'Not yet, but I want to get them.'

Lost in thought about the cars that they had just mentioned, Caesar lit a cigarette, his first for the day, and then offered Jimmy one, who graciously accepted.

'I can't smoke in the car, can I?' asked Caesar hopefully.

'I don't think it should be a problem,' replied Jimmy coolly.

Both men got in with cigarettes in their mouths and Jimmy handed the driver the address of their destination. They were returning to Nakamura Motors to talk to the manager. The windows in the car were almost all the way up, leaving only a small gap at the top for the circulation of air.

The drive took the men through the beautiful parts of the upper city, even across the exotic Park Woods, and then down the beach where Jimmy jealously watched teenagers having fun in the ocean and playing volleyball on the soft sand. Caesar saw this and let out a little knowing chuckle as he knew that one day Jimmy would also be mature enough to realize that the reason they worked was so that they could do things like buy private beaches and act like teenagers again. With the ridiculous sums of money that flowed through the banking sector of this region, the income of everyone who was even remotely associated with a bank was always a grand amount.

The car pulled up as it had the day before and this was followed by the two men getting out, letting their half-finished cigarettes drop from their mouth to the floor and then get stubbed out under their shoes. Caesar took the lead while approaching the showroom and he was glad to see people inside, ensuring him that it was open. Even though it was still morning, the guard who had spoken to them yesterday had continued to sleep on the job today and both men wondered why the manager had hired him.

Entering the grand showroom, both men temporarily forgot about the task at hand and got lost in the exotic cars that surrounded them. They seemed alien in design yet intensely familiar at the same time. The main attraction of the showroom rested on a certain high platform that rotated about four feet above the ground. This brought the headlights of the car up to the eye-line of the average customer.

The manager approached the two men and asked them as he had usually asked hundreds of customers, no thousands before, 'How may I help you?'

Since Jimmy was only here to provide technical information, Caesar took the lead, 'We're here from the Royal Citizen's Bank. Mind if we talk in your office?'

'Sure,' murmured the manager thoughtfully and then led the two men through the showroom. Usually Caesar would have used this time to study the man, but he was too distracted by the lovely cars in the showroom. Jimmy acted the same and he even went as far as to hope that Caesar would ask him to wait outside so that he could take more time to look at all these cars.

The trio, led by the manager, arrived at a door with a sign that read Mr Johnson on the door. Noticing this, Caesar realized that this man probably would have only minimal power and he would have to go and see the owner to talk about the account.

The three men entered and Caesar and Jimmy took their seats across Mr Johnson when they were indicated to do so.

'So, what can I do for you gentlemen?'

'We're here representing the Royal Citizen's Bank.' Caesar planned to do all the talking.

'Yeah, that's what's confusing me. I thought we dealt with IXL.'

'Yes, but the IXL bank shut down recently. So we would like to talk about taking on the account of Nakamura Motors.'

'Oh! Well I certainly don't have that kind of authority. The most I can do is sign off on overdraft payments.'

'So who should we talk to about this?'

'Well the firm's only called Nakamura Motors on paper. Everyone refers to it as Nakamura Premium Cars or NPC otherwise. The firm was recently sold by Mr Nakamura to Red Sun Industries.'

'Red Sun Industries? I've never heard of it.'

'I'm not surprised. It's not based in this country.'

'Are you serious? It was sold to an international buyer?'

'Yes, in the Nakazato District.'

'This just got way harder than I expected it to be.'

Caesar and Jimmy got up and nodded a thank you to the manager. They then left the showroom quietly and walked back to the car. In fact, Caesar was annoyed enough to stop and light a cigarette in front of a rather large no-smoking sign. Jimmy had never understood why someone would rebel in such a way, but knew well enough not to say anything. Everyone had their own way of dealing with frustration.

In the car, Caesar smoked quietly and studied the situation mentally. Jimmy, on the other hand, remained more pro-active and decided to call Mulligan. He dialled the call and a few moments later, his boss answered.

'What's going on Jimmy?'

'Sir, there was a slight problem with Nakamura Motors.'

'Did Brookstone already get to them?'

'No, nothing like that. It turns out that the owner,

Mr Nakamura, sold the firm off to a company called Red Sun Industries.'

'Red Sun Industries? I've never heard of it.'

'It's not local. It's based out of the Nakazato District.'

'Damn it. Come straight to my office. I'll figure out our plan till then.'

The call ended.

The situation had gone from easy to ugly. Mulligan had believed that Nakamura Motors would have been an easy win and with Thornton Plumbing already on the roster, victory was within easy reach. This development, however, had made it difficult to ensure the lead.

The first thing to do would be to get more information. He buzzed his secretary and was greeted with an efficient voice on the other end, 'What do you need sir?'

'Put me through to our branch in the Nakazato District.'

'The Nakazato District sir?'

'Yes and make it quick.'

The phone was put down and Mulligan took another drag from a lit cigarette that lay on the edge of his ashtray. He was on edge. He tried to divert his mind as he waited for the call by looking at the latest share values of some of his biggest clients. The large number of green arrows pointing up turned his anxiety into a smile. At least some things were going well.

The phone buzzed again and Mulligan quickly answered.

'Did you get through?'

'No sir. I do, however, have the Chairman on the line wanting to talk to you.'

'Put him through.'

There was a click and a slide. Then Mulligan heard the classic voice of Chairman on the other end.

'Mr Mulligan, I believe you are enquiring about our branch in the Nakazato District.'

'Yes, sir. Is that an issue?'

'Not exactly. As you already must know, the Nakazato District is home to an extremely competitive business environment. Well, as it turns out, the management of our local branch in that area was not competent enough to survive and that lead us to shutting the branch down about five weeks ago.'

'Well sir, this really isn't something that I was expecting.'

'I'm not surprised. So why were you enquiring about that branch anyway?'

'Well sir, there's a company called Red Sun Industries, based out of that area and we needed information on it. We wish to pursue one of their local ventures as a potential client.'

'Listen to me close, Mulligan. Red Sun Industries is a massive firm that we've had our eye on for a long time. I'm going to send you all the information, but only on one condition. If you go after this firm, you better get the whole deal and not just the venture.'

'Sir, do you honestly think that it would be possible for a firm that size to rely solely on an international banker?'

'It is possible. So do you want to go after Red Sun Industries or should I send someone else?'

'Sir, I actually believe that Caesar would be the right man for this job.'

'Good thinking, Mulligan. Put him on the next plane to the Nakazato District.'

'It'll be done sir.'

By the time Caesar arrived to meet Mulligan twenty minutes later, he had no idea as to how much had happened while he had been sitting idly in the car.

The three men sat in Mulligan's office with cigarettes in their mouths. Jimmy felt guilty that he had started smoking regularly, but felt that it was almost impossible not to do so while spending so much time with someone as infectious as his boss or Caesar. As the three men sat in silence, simply cherishing the nicotine and tobacco in their systems, the phone buzzed and broke the peaceful silence.

Mulligan picked it up and his secretary answered a request that he had made only a few minutes ago, 'sir I have purchased a seat on a flight to the Nakazato District for today. It leaves at 11.15 pm.'

'First class?'

'Of course sir. Also, a speed-mail file has arrived from the Head Office. Should I print it out and bring it over to you?'

'That would be perfect.'

Mulligan put the phone down and then decided to address the curious and complicated faces of the two men who sat across him.

'What's going on boss?' asked Jimmy.

'I spoke to the Chairman after you called me and there has been a rather interesting development. He wants us to go after Red Sun Industries as a whole and not just their venture.' Mulligan tried to maintain a matter-of-fact tone.

Caesar stubbed out his cigarette and then asked, 'Wouldn't that be in the jurisdiction of our local branch in that area?'

Mulligan revealed a grim expression and replied, 'Well it turns out that our branch in the Nakazato District went under recently so it's now our responsibility to get that account. The Chairman and I both thought that it would be best if it was you who went after the firm. I would have come with you, but I have to deal with Brookstone back here.'

A deep thoughtful silence plagued the room. A knock on the door, however, quickly interrupted this.

'Come in,' ordered Mulligan from behind his desk.

The secretary stepped in carrying a folder labeled 'Red Sun Industries' and placed it on the table. She then received a simple indicative nod from Mulligan and left the room.

Mulligan pushed the folder towards Caesar and spoke coolly, 'Your flight leaves at eleven-fifteen tonight. First class. We're depending on you.'

Mulligan and Jimmy stubbed out their cigarettes and then Caesar got up from his chair and lifted the folder. 'Don't worry. I'll take care of it by the end of the week.' His voice shimmered with confidence.

'Jimmy, give us a minute will you?' asked Mulligan politely.

The kid nodded and left the room leaving Caesar waiting for what Mulligan had to say.

'I was hoping,' began Mulligan with a tone of friendliness, 'that you would do me a favour. I need you to structure an account so that Nakamura Motors comes to this branch while the rest of Red Sun Industries goes to the Head Office. I can't handle an entire international firm right now and I only need Nakamura Motors to ensure that I remain ahead of Brookstone.'

Caesar chuckled. He was impressed by the frankness of his boss. 'Sure thing.'

Both men shook hands and then Caesar left the room. A sense of heavy responsibility now rested on the man's shoulders. To fail to obtain this account would mean to fail Mulligan as well as the Chairman, and that was something that Caesar feared more than death.

Caesar sat on Seat 2C in the first class cabin and as it was an aisle seat, he realized how much better it was to have a window one instead. The Nakazato District was approximately two hours away by plane and he had decided that it would be best to use this time to go over the folder that Mulligan had given him instead of just wasting time watching an in-flight movie.

The plane took off and Caesar felt the hefty Airbus A380 soar through the air. After the 'Fasten Your Seatbelt' sign stopped blinking, one of the air-hostesses passed by and he quickly stopped her and asked for a glass of wine.

The folder labelled 'Red Sun Industries' contained nothing more than the usual accounting data that Caesar usually found in such folders. A glance through the cash-flow forecasts and balance sheets only showed what the man already knew and that was that this firm was a rich one. Besides owning Nakamura Motors, Red Sun Industries seemed to maintain its primary focus on the manufacturing and sale of production equipment. Some of their big customers included extremely large car and computer manufacturers and Caesar was clearly more than a little impressed.

Two long and boring hours later, the plane touched down on the tarmac and Caesar was annoyed that he couldn't catch a glimpse of the city as the plane had begun to descend. He started to realize how much he underappreciated the value of the window seat. According to him, the people who maintained a defence that aisle seats were better than window seats were senseless and he could never truly sympathize with their point of view. It always had something to do with the bathroom.

Thirty minutes after landing and explaining to the immigration officer exactly what it was that he did, Caesar found himself sitting in the back of a luxury sedan being driven through the streets of the greater Nakazato District area. He had failed to see what kind of car it was from the outside, but the level of comfort implied that it was probably a Bentley or a Rolls Royce.

The car had been sent by the Golden Palm Hotel, the hotel where he planned to stay during his visit to the Nakazato District. The name had come off as odd initially because the word 'Palm' in a hotel usually implied close proximity to the beach. The Nakazato District, however, was a completely landlocked area. Upon further inquiry, information had been gained that the hotel had been named Golden Palm as it was a part of an international chain.

The car pulled up in front of the hotel and Caesar got out. Looking back at the vehicle, he saw that his guess had been correct as the car was a classic-looking Bentley. Unusually, he couldn't make out the model, but that was probably because he didn't have too much of an interest in luxury cars. His department was sports and exotic goods.

Some bellhops grabbed his bags from the trunk of his car while a waiter offered him a glass of icewater. Caesar then stepped into the lobby and was quickly led by what he could only make out to be some sort of doorman to the reception where yet another man greeted him with a smile. The unbalanced ratio of the number of male and female employees indicated a heavily regressive cultural backdrop.

'Mr Caesar from the Royal Citizen's Bank, right?' asked the receptionist before he could even sit down.

'Yes.'

'Well, everything's taken care of sir. Kurohagi here will take you up to your room and answer any questions you might have.'

Kurohagi seemed like yet another hotel worker. Caesar

couldn't guess what the title stood for, but he didn't seem that important. He was standing next to the receptionist with an unnatural smile on his face and upon hearing his name, he had handed Caesar a key and now led the way to the elevator.

After a quiet elevator ride and an unnecessary introduction to the 'majestic' features of the room, Kurohagi handed Caesar two magnetic keys, received a gracious tip and then left the guest alone. Finally by himself, Caesar jumped into the shower and then curled up under the blanket, dressed only in a shiny red silk robe.

He flicked on the television and found nothing but a lot of movie channels that were in every language, but English. After scrolling through some forty channels, however, a news channel that had English subtitles was found and Caesar watched intently. In ten minutes, however, he was sick of reading badly punctuated subtitles and decided to get down to business. He opened the folder that he had been carrying in his arm since he had landed and found the office number for Red Sun Industries.

He lifted the receiver on the hotel phone and punched in the number. The number started to dial and Caesar checked the local time. It was six thirty. Even with the time difference, he was probably too late to get an appointment for tomorrow. Deciding to forget about business for today and in turn focus on enjoying the local delights of the Nakazato District, Caesar got dressed in a beige suit and white shirt and then headed down to the lobby.

The concierge informed him about some local touristy attractions that ranged from carnivals to nightclubs, but none of them seemed appealing. So, instead, he stepped out of the hotel and took a stroll down the road and around the block.

It didn't take him long to realize the reason as to why there were such few pedestrians. The Nakazato District was not a walking city. Everything from the uncontrollable pollution to the scorching heat and humidity made for extremely unpleasant conditions for a walk. Returning to the hotel, the concierge let out a knowing chuckle and Caesar took it in good humor.

'I can see why you suggested the hotel car.'

'Well sir, I don't want to say, I told you so.'

'So, I suddenly want to go to someplace really cold.'

'Well there's an ice bar, a couple of blocks away.'

'What's it called?'

'Shinto's.'

'Alright. That sounds good. Can you please ready a hotel car to take me there? I'm going to go up and change into a fresh shirt.'

'I would suggest cotton.'

Caesar let out a chuckle and walked away. Ten minutes later, he was back in the lobby looking much fresher than before. He strolled towards the concierge who handed him a tag for the hotel car and then walked out onto the porch.

This time the hotel car turned out to be a black Lamborghini Gallardo and even though Caesar marvelled at the car, it was clearly an extremely odd choice for a hotel to have a two-door car available for guests.

The driver got out and spoke apologetically, 'I'm sorry sir. This was the only car that hadn't already been booked. Will it be okay or should I call a car service?'

Caesar let out a chuckle and asked coyly, 'It'll be okay if I'm the one who drives.'

The driver, who wasn't expecting such a request, looked

at the head valet who gave him a nod.

He then turned his attention back to Caesar who was still appreciating the car and replied, 'Sure sir.'

Excited, Caesar got into the car while the driver got in beside him. He then jammed down the accelerator and at 60 kmph, drove out of the hotel and on the street, he instantly hit 200. The driver held on for his life as Caesar swerved the car in and out of traffic with no destination in mind.

'This has some serious horsepower,' he said, finally bringing the car down to normal speed. He had had his fun.

'Yes it does sir. Please drive slower next time.' The driver was nearly begging.

'So how do I get to Shinto's?'

For the next ten minutes, Caesar drove around the area following the driver's instructions and then they finally arrived at a shady-looking entrance, leading down to a basement.

'That's the bar?' asked Caesar unsurely.

'Yes sir,' replied the driver making no attempt to reassure him.

'Okay. I'm going to be here for a couple of hours and I'm sure as hell going to drink. So what I want you to do is, go back to the hotel and come back with a four-door as soon as you can.'

'Okay sir.'

Caesar got out of the car and then walked through the door and down the damp staircase that lead to the main bar. Upon finally reaching the bottom of the staircase, and getting a look at the bar itself, he almost instantly realized why the place came recommended and what an ice bar was.

Compared to the dark and damp forty steps he had just descended, the bright glow of the bar itself came as a welcome surprise. The contrast took everyone who ever walked into the bar, for the first time, by surprise and whoever had designed the place clearly seemed to have a knack for doing good work.

The large bar seemed more like a nightclub and Caesar wondered if the name Shinto's came from the owner being named Shinto or if it meant something else. This unusual question began to unsettle him as everywhere he looked all he could see was a large amount of bright white signs that read SHINTO'S.

It being referred to as an 'Ice Bar' probably came from the fact that it was freezing cold in here and there was literally, a lot of ice everywhere. Just by the exit point of the staircase, two ice sculptures of princesses rested meaningfully. The floor was also bright white marble with the occasional black carpet that echoed the pitch black night sky painted ceiling.

The music in the room was louder than most clubs and Caesar wondered as to how on earth one would go about ordering a drink. After observing the customers, however, it seemed that nobody was having too much difficulty doing so and he wondered if this bar, like many other clubs that he had been to, required the employees to learn how to lip read. A simple initiative that would save the voices of countless customers who would have attempted to scream over the music, otherwise.

Walking around the bar and observing the acoustic changes, Caesar also noticed that the music that was being played was highly unusual. He was used to hearing pop and house music when he would walk into a club and, in the most irregular cases, maybe some trance or classic rhythm and base. But what he heard being played at Shinto's was something that he had only heard rumours about.

It was an epic blend of rock and pop called Eurobeat that was derived from mid-European regions during the eighties and, while mostly forgotten about, this music had developed a core following in certain Asian countries. The constant pulsating rhythm with not a single off-time note and contrasting relaxed light female singing really got Caesar thinking about what a great song this was and within minutes he was hooked and eagerly waiting for the DJ to play the next exciting track.

Besides the bar and alcohol itself, another grasping aspect of Shinto's seemed to be the overly colourful dance floor. The dance floor was much larger than usual and was at least thirty feet by thirty feet. The floor was divided into about ten different glass sections that lit up in different colours at a rapid rate. All of the colours were excessively bright and ranged from pink to green to yellow. Just looking at it would get someone's heart beating faster.

The crowd that occupied the floor and the rest of the bar was mostly extremely young and barely legal. Ranging from their early twenties to the early thirties, Caesar felt as though he was probably the oldest person there and didn't feel as welcome as earlier. Looking around though, he was greeted with a lot of alcohol-induced smiles and saw that almost every male was wearing a dark black suit. The girls, however, were dressed in everything from short-skirts and t-shirts to full-blown formal dresses.

Caesar stood leaning against a wall and watched people dance with an equilateral sense that was probably derived from the engaging music. His intense thought process was shattered, however, as he was approached by a man dressed in a white suit and black shirt. He was about 6 feet 4 inches and had a thick moustache. Almost instantly, he stood out from the crowd and Caesar could only guess as to who he was.

'Can I help you?' asked the man in the white suit kindly.

'Yes, I was just having a look around. A truly exciting place, this is. I would like to speak to the DJ.'

'Why?'

'Well, I've never heard this music before and I was wondering if he would sell me one of his CD's.'

'Well that shouldn't be a problem. Welcome to Shinto's, by the way. I should have probably said that to you earlier. Would you like a table?'

'Some sort of private booth would be better.'

The man in the white suit escorted Caesar through the perplexingly amazing club and then stopped in front of a small secluded area.

'This here is the best we can do in terms of privacy.'

'It's perfectly okay.'

'Are you alone tonight?'

'Yes.'

'Please have a seat and I'll have something to drink sent over for you. What would you like?'

'Four or five of your best cocktails.'

'Lovely.'

Caesar got settled into his booth and as the man began to walk away, he asked innocently, 'Are you the manager?'

'No, I'm Shinto,' replied the man as he turned around and winked.

Caesar smiled and moments later, found himself facing five different local delicacies. The waitress had brought the drinks over to his table at an astounding speed, and left without asking for a tip. This place had won his approval ten times over.

Starting from the left, Caesar started to study his drinks.

The first one was crimson in colour and had more ice cubes in it than a man could count. The darker colour, at the bottom, indicated a heavy alcohol base, but the lemon wedge on the top gave the drink a peachy feel. By the end of it, it was clear that the drink had more than a little alcohol and the lemon wedge simply softened the taste.

The next three drinks were vastly similar. It was more or less the same drink in three different flavors to be exact but nonetheless, a good three flavors they were. The first one was orange and since Caesar had never liked oranges, he thought he would have hated the drink. It turned out, however, that alcohol has the amazing ability to take even the worst of drinks and make them likable. The next two flavors were apple and strawberry. Both were good in their own way with strawberry taking the prize for the sweetest alcoholic drink ever made.

The last and final drink was of a black colour and since the only black coloured drink that Caesar had even seen was a soda, he was excited to find out what the colour held within it. What initially tasted like a horrible mixture of rat poison and other forms of liquid death, the drink actually quickly grew on him and he found himself enjoying the last few sips.

As he put the last glass back on the table and realized that he had just finished drinking five different alcohol-heavy drinks, the man's vision blurred and the Eurobeat music conquered his mind. His foot started tapping and he then got up to head to the dance floor. It was going to be a long night of partying at Shinto's.

Hello, Goodbye

Waking up still dressed in last night's suit, and finding a Eurobeat CD lying on his bedside table, Caesar knew he had gotten carried away last night. Without thinking, he had a shower and then popped a few pills for his headache. He then noticed that it was probably too bright outside for it to still be morning and was proven right when he checked his watch and found out the time to be two in the afternoon.

The first thing he did was to get down to business. He was in the Nakazato District for a reason after all. He dialled the number in the folder and exactly three rings later, he was greeted by the voice of a professional secretary, 'Red Sun Industries. How may I help you?'

'Hello. I'm from the Royal Citizen's Bank and I would like a meeting with…' Caesar realized he didn't know the name of the owner and quickly sifted through folder to find it. Moments passed as the secretary patiently waited.

'Meeting with who sir?'

Caesar found the name and answered, 'Mr Yoshiro.'

'Okay. Let me check with him. Would you like to hold or should I call back?'

'I'll hold.'

Silent minutes passed once again, but this time it was Caesar who was doing the patient waiting.

'You can come by in an hour. The office is on the fiftieth floor of our building. Please don't be late.'

Caesar hung up and then dialled the concierge who picked up instantly.

'Concierge. How may I help you?'

'How far is the Red Sun Industries building?'

'Their head office or factory office?'

'Head Office.'

'About thirty minutes during this time of the day.'

'Can you have a car ready for me to head there in about fifteen minutes? Please make sure that it's a sedan and the driver knows the way.'

'Won't be a problem, sir.'

Caesar hung up and then realized he was starving. He walked up to the mini-bar, which was curiously under the television, and then picked out everything eatable from the selection. He scarfed down the food and then put on a plain black suit with a black tie. Five minutes later, he was downstairs on the porch, waiting for the hotel car to pull up.

Fortunately, this time the car was the same that had brought him from the airport and Caesar quickly hopped into the backseat of the Bentley. The driver smiled at Caesar and then asked, 'Should I take the scenic view? We can drive past the Red Sun Industries Factory if you would like.'

A gracious proposition, but one Caesar rejected nonetheless, 'I'm in a hurry actually so straight to the Head Office would be fine. Also, I need to smoke in the car, would that be a problem?'

'Not at all sir. Just roll down the window.'

Caesar did as he was asked to and then lit a cigarette after what he felt like was a millennium.

The drive was more or less a solemn one with Caesar's only objectives being to fulfill his desire for nicotine and tobacco while enjoying the sights of the Nakazato District as much as he could.

Thirty-five minutes later, the car pulled up in front of a tall white building that had a massive sign reading 'Red Sun Industries,' on top. Next to it was a logo of a sun gleaming down on a wrench.

Caesar told the driver to wait and then walked into the ground floor of the office building. Ignoring any staff that tried to make eye contact with him, he walked straight to the elevator of the male-dominated office and waited for it to open. As it did, twelve more male office workers, each of whom were on their phone, poured out of the elevator and further added to the already densely populated floor.

He got into the elevator as soon as it became vacant and then hoped with all his heart that no one would join him. His wish was granted and he then hit the button for the fiftieth floor and headed straight up. He checked his watch and even with the best of his effort, he was already four minutes late.

The doors opened and revealed a gleaming floor, which only served the purpose of housing one office. Looking outside, Caesar also noticed that this was the top floor of the building and its height allowed for a beautiful view of the Nakazato District. He walked across the carpeted floors and approached the wooden door that read 'Mr Yoshiro'. It wasn't a glamorous sign, but it managed to convey the epic importance of the man by entrapping the magnificence of the rest of the floor.

Caesar pushed through the door and as expected, he entered a waiting room where a secretary greeted him with a smile. He took a seat on the sofa and then spoke calmly,

'I'm from the Royal Citizen's Bank. Sorry for being late.' He was as charming as ever.

The secretary replied with wide smile, 'Don't worry about it. Mr Yoshiro is still in a meeting so it'll be a few minutes.'

Caesar nodded and settled more comfortably into the sofa.

The wait didn't last for much longer, however, as the door swung open and a woman dressed in a black dress and high heels, unusual for the afternoon, stepped out of the office and walked past Caesar.

'Go right ahead,' said the secretary and he did as he was told.

Caesar pushed through the door and entered one of the most lavish offices he had ever seen. Beautiful, white Italian marble flooring and wooden walls created a light yet dense atmosphere in the room. On either wall, large scale wooden shelves were occupied by dozens of volumes of serialized files that made a strong working impression on whoever entered the office.

In the middle of the office was the main desk and behind the desk was what made the office truly amazing. A large scale semi-circular window occupied the entire wall and gave the visitor a sensation of being connected with the beauty of the Nakazato District itself. The light blue skies hovered overhead and a beautiful unblinking horizon could be seen in the distance.

The table itself, a grand affair, had a leather mat on top with a lot of gold pens lying around. The paperwork on the desk itself, however, was at a bare minimum with only a soft pile on the left side. The wooden premium design shined across the invasive sunlight and acted as an impressive means to further awe anyone who ever stepped into the office.

The emperor of the room, Mr Yoshiro, sat behind his grand desk with a still expression that was perfect for any situation. He was an elderly looking man but as Caesar's files had revealed to him, was only in his late forties in reality. From the bad skin to his dead eyes, it could only be assumed that the man had probably spent a lot of time in the sun and was familiar with a lot of smoking.

Yoshiro sat on a super-sized black leather chair, not the type with wheels, but more of a classic design. The fact that it seemed brand new probably meant that it was, or maybe its youthful appearance was derived from the fact that Mr Yoshiro didn't spend too much time in his office. All things considered, the first possibility seemed more likely.

The man in the chair was dressed in a white suit; one that was extremely similar to the one Caesar had seen Shinto wearing, and a black shirt. No tie was around the man's collar and the top two buttons hung loose, revealing a hairless chest. His head was full of white hair that was pulled back and if people didn't know any better, he would probably be assumed to be yakuza instead of a world-class businessman.

Yoshiro made an indication with his hand and Caesar settled into a comfortable chair across him.

'I am Takumi Yoshiro,' announced the owner of the firm with majestic humbleness.

'I know who you are Mr Yoshiro. We, at the Royal Citizen's Bank, have considered your firm for approach for quite some time now.'

'Didn't the local branch of your bank shut down?'

'Yes it did.'

'So you have flown internationally to grace me with your presence?'

'Yes. We believe that a firm of this stature deserves a personal touch.'

'Well, I'm flattered. But I have to be honest with you, banking our money internationally doesn't seem to be appealing, especially with such high-quality local institutions available to us. Also, the fact that your local branch failed to survive isn't exactly overwhelming me with faith towards your bank.'

'I can understand your doubts sir, but I would like you to know that our local endeavour was only regressed because of an opportunity to flourish in a different area. What was supposed to be a simple relocation was quickly looked upon as a sign of weakness by our friends and rivals alike; quite pitiful to be brutally honest.'

'Relocation? You certainly have a way with words young man. But excuses don't do much for me. Why don't you give me an actual reason to shift the company's wealth to your bank?'

'Well sir, if you decided to take up the opportunity to let us protect your assets, we would be able to offer you a variety of benefits. The most important of these benefits would be the fact that the interest rate offered in our country is almost double than that offered in the Nakazato District. You get six per cent per annum here, but where we are offering to place your money, you could get as much as twelve to fourteen per cent, based on the year.'

'Red Sun Industries has had some problems with local institutions in the past and your offer seems even more appealing with the interest rate, but the truth of the matter is that my concern lies elsewhere. First, since the money won't be available locally, transfer of payments may take much longer than what is suitable for us. Also, the exchange rate can cause serious problems for us if our currency appreciates too much or yours depreciates too much. The value of our money is, for obvious reasons, a major reason as to why we haven't decided to bank internationally.'

'Fortunately enough sir, I have planned for these possible mishaps, and solutions have already been accommodated. Payments will never be delayed as long as we have been informed at least fourteen hours in advance. In case of emergencies, the personal contact numbers of certain high-level personnel will be available to you for immediate transfer of sums up to the value of two million dollars. On the other hand, we are in a slight predicament when it comes to the exchange rate issue. The best we can offer is that thirty per cent of your account will be maintained in your local currency.'

'Your planning impresses me greatly. I can see why the Royal Citizen's Bank has been successful all these years. I'll tell you what, if you can assure me that fifty per cent, not thirty, of our account will be maintained in our local currency, you can have our account.'

'Done.'

'Good. Now the only other thing that is left for you to do is to get the paperwork signed. There is a slight difficulty with that, however.'

'What's the difficulty, sir?'

'Well, as you might already know, Red Sun Industries is owned by me and my brother, Hideo Yoshiro equally. So to go through with this movement of money, you will need to get his signature as well.'

'Will that be a problem?'

'My brother is in prison.'

'On what charge?'

'Murder. Nothing financial. He killed a police officer.'

'My god. So I'll have to go to prison to get his signature on the paperwork?'

'Yes.'

Caesar got up from his chair and took a long breath. The situation had just gotten more complicated than it needed to be. He, however, managed to maintain a composed expression and then spoke calmly, 'I'll get the paperwork sent to me by tomorrow. How should we do the rest?'

Takumi Yoshiro took a long breath and then explained the simple process as he had a number of times before. 'Come by here in the morning and I'll sign the paper. Then go to the state prison during visiting hours to meet my brother. As we already have agreed upon, he will sign the paper as soon as he sees my signature. There shouldn't be a problem.'

Caesar nodded in a way that suggested that he understood the situation. But the truth was that he didn't. Why hadn't the brother simply given the extra one per cent to Mr Yoshiro? That would have given the other man all the majority control and made life much simpler for everyone. Caesar, however, remembered that some people lived of control and maybe Hideo Yoshiro was one of them.

An hour later, Caesar was back in his hotel room, sitting on the balcony with a cigarette in his mouth. Smoke filtered into his lungs every ninety seconds and with every drag, he felt as though he was getting closer to understanding the situation between the Yoshiro brothers. It was truly quite a dysfunctional way of dealing with things.

Half an hour later, Caesar decided to get down to work. He pulled out his phone and dialled for Mulligan's office. A long time passed as the phone seemed to ring endlessly, but the call was finally answered by the secretary and then put through.

'Is it important? I'm on my way home otherwise,' said Mulligan as he answered the phone grumpily.

'Yes, it is. Turns out Takumi Yoshiro only owns fifty per cent of the company. The other half is owned by his brother who's rotting in jail for killing a cop.'

'How do you know this?'

'Yoshiro told me himself. They've agreed to the deal, but you might want to cross check it with the Chairman once, before we go through with it.'

'Alright, I'll get to it. I'll call you back as soon as I can with a decision. Stay put.'

The call ended. Caesar wasn't planning to go anywhere. He was enjoying his cigarette under the looming sun of dusk.

Back at the regional office, Mulligan settled deeper into his chair. What would have been a flawless day had just been ruined by something that he should have caught up on a while ago. Remembering the file information, however, he didn't feel as guilty anymore as all the folder had said was 'Yoshiro maintains complete ownership'. No one could have known what that really meant.

Stubbing out his last cigarette for the working day, Mulligan picked up his phone and reluctantly ordered his secretary, 'Connect me to the Chairman please.'

'Sure sir,' was the expected reply he got and was then put on hold.

Minutes passed as Mulligan listened to the monotone of the hold line while he studied the situation in his mind. The call was then finally picked up and the Chairman answered indifferently, 'What is it?'

'Sir, its Mulligan here. About the Red Sun Industries account, there's been a development that needs your attention.'

'What's going on?'

'Well, it turns out that half of the firm is owned by Hideo Yoshiro who is in prison for committing homicide. They have agreed to doing business with us, however, I wanted to know if we are still keen to do business with them. The owner being in jail can have serious fiscal ramifications in the future.'

'I was already aware of this situation. Hideo Yoshiro is a harmless man. Go through with the deal.'

'Thank you for your time sir.'

The call ended, but instead of putting the receiver down, Mulligan just called Caesar instead. Almost instantly, the phone was answered.

'Did you talk to the Chairman?' asked Caesar eagerly.

'Yes I did. He says he knew about the situation all along and wants to go through with it anyway. I'll send you the paperwork as soon as I can. Did they agree to the figures we had set?'

'Yeah for the most part they did. There's only a small change. Their asset holdings in local currency have to be fifty per cent. Not thirty.'

'That'll make life difficult for Head Office, but at least you got the account. Good job.'

The last business phone call for the night finally ended and Caesar let out a sigh of relief. Things had gone much better than he had expected. He then walked to the in-room stereo and plugged in the Eurobeat CD that he had bought from the DJ. The sound came on and the pulsating rhythm of the music elevated the listener to a heavenly level.

The next morning, Caesar woke up and found a brown

packet waiting for him. Upon opening it, he found the contract that he had asked Mulligan to send and after studying it drowsily for a few seconds, he put it aside and took a shower. Since today was a good day, Caesar decided to get dressed in a light blue suit with a white shirt. The bright sun forced him to wear sunglasses and, all in all, today felt like a good day.

Heading down to the lobby with the contract under his arm, Caesar wondered what his visit to the state prison would be like and whether he would have to convince Hideo as he had his brother. Takumi Yoshiro had been reassuring, however, there was no doubt that things would go smoothly.

The elevator doors opened and Caesar strolled through the lobby. He was handed a car tag by the concierge. Upon stepping out onto the porch, he found that the tag entitled him to be driven around in a black hotel-owned Lexus. Settling in comfortably and placing the contract to his side, Caesar rolled down the window and lit a cigarette. He even asked the driver to take the scenic route so that he could get a glimpse of the Red Sun Industries Factory from the outside.

Takumi Yoshiro, in so many words, had expressed that he could drop by any time and Caesar hoped to take advantage of that offer today. He had scheduled his whole day well. After meeting and signing with Takumi, Caesar would still have a good four hours to go to the prison and get Hideo's signature.

Twenty minutes later, Caesar found himself being driven past the Red Sun Industries Factory and from the look of it; it was clearly a very large structure. The fact that there was no visible smoke emanating from the factory was a good environmental sign and upon questioning the driver, Caesar also found out that there was no river to pollute nearby either. Even though he wasn't counting on it, Caesar was glad that the firm had cut down on possible external costs even though it may have been at a heavy personal expense.

After the drive past the factory, the driver turned up the speed and soon, they arrived at the Head Office. Caesar got out and strolled through the lobby as he had done the day before and then entered the elevator. This time he wasn't lucky enough to be alone and was instead stuffed in with ten other male workers.

After almost an endless journey, the elevator arrived at the top floor and Caesar got out. He walked through the first door and entered the waiting area where he was flashed a look of concern by the secretary. This was probably because he didn't have a meeting fixed today and judging by the high occupancy of the waiting room, he probably wouldn't have gotten one in normal circumstances either.

The secretary approached him and said, 'sir, I see that you aren't on the agenda today and I must say that Mr Yoshiro's day is quite full. It would be best if you came back with an appointment some other time.'

Caesar smiled charmingly and replied, 'Don't worry about it. Just let Mr Yoshiro know that I'm here and he'll meet me. We only have a small piece of business to attend to.'

As asked for, the secretary informed Mr Yoshiro of Caesar's presence as soon as the current visitor left the office and he was instantly invited in. Entering the glamorous office for the second time, Caesar didn't feel as awe-struck as he had felt the day before.

The man took his seat and was almost instantly asked, 'Did you bring the contract?'

Caesar smiled and replied, 'Yes I did.' He then pulled it out and placed it on the table.

Yoshiro flipped through it and then pressed a button on his phone. Minutes later, a young looking, healthy man entered the room and picked up the contract.

Upon seeing Caesar's confusion, Yoshiro explained calmly, 'This here is Mr Fujiwara, my lawyer. I just need him to go over it once before I can sign it.'

Minutes passed as Fujiwara went through the document. During this time, Caesar stared out the grand window across him while Yoshiro flipped through some documents.

'It looks okay,' announced Fujiwara a while later. He then watched closely as both Caesar and his boss signed the document.

After the signing, Caesar picked up the contract and then asked for instructions on how to conduct the next step, 'Mr Yoshiro, will your brother agree to this for sure?'

Fujiwara heard the question and then after being flashed a look by his boss, left the room. Caesar's question was then answered, 'Just head down to the Nakazato District C. C. C. and sign up on the visitor's list. There might be a twenty-minute wait, but after that, you'll be taken to see my brother. If the warden comes around and questions you, stay calm and give him my name.'

Caesar nodded his head as he took in all these facts and then replied, 'I understand. What does C. C. C. stand for though?'

Yoshiro looked at the man across him with confused eyes and answered sharply, 'Criminal Containment Center, of course.'

Having his curiosity satisfied, Caesar got up and shook hands with Yoshiro. He then left the office and minutes later, was in the car being driven around in the hotel Lexus. The driver looked back at his client and asked professionally, 'Back to the hotel, sir?'

Caesar shook his head and replied, 'Head to the Nakazato District Criminal Containment Center.'

Upon hearing this extremely unusual request, the driver flashed a look of confusion and doubt, but then remembered that it was not his business to judge where his clients wanted to go. All he had to do was drive them.

Ten minutes passed and Caesar sat in the back seat of the car with a cigarette in his hand. As he enjoyed the sights of everyday activity in a foreign area, he asked the driver a question that reflected his rare impatient side, 'How much longer?'

The driver took a breath and replied calmly, 'About thirty-five minutes, sir.'

As stated, the driver pulled up in front of the visitor's parking lot of the Nakazato District Criminal Containment Center, exactly thirty-five minutes later. The parking lot was filled with litter and the cars that were improperly parked around clearly showed a certain side of the area that Caesar hadn't had the privilege of witnessing before.

On the outside, the prison was a painting of grim brutality. Only two stories tall, the prison covered a wide area to make up for its short height. The difference in the quality of buildings made it easy to determine which parts were in the original plan while differentiating the parts that had been added as modifications or expansions. Painted in a colour of unattractive charcoal, the building made no attempt to attract attention to itself and even the sign that stated 'Nakazato District C. C. C.' was written in dull white colour.

Caesar got out of the car and stepped out onto the damp pavement below. He then walked up a flight of cheap metallic steps that led to a poorly designed security-door with a label reading 'Visitation' on top. Pushing through, he entered into a room that was filled with more correctional officers than he could count. The officers were screening every visitor, whether child or spouse, in detail and numerous signs on the wall read 'No Metal, No Glass, No Liquid'.

The first step of the screening process was a simple metal detector. Caesar stepped through it and upon its rapid beeping, one of the officers approached him and flashed him an annoyed look. He was then made to move through the detector again and this time it didn't beep. It was clearly a faulty device. Caesar had come planned for the security check and, therefore, the only items he had on him was a plastic pen, his clothes and the contract.

The next step of the process was a hand-searching of the man's pockets and clothes. Even though he felt slightly violated, Caesar let it slide and bravely moved on to the next harrowing stage of the journey. The grim interior of grey walls and floors didn't exactly brighten up the mood either.

The next stage was a simple one where all Caesar had to do was take of his shoes for them to be searched. The process was quickly completed and then a burly office grabbed him by the arm and dragged him out to the main visitation area.

The main visitation area was pretty much just a really long line of cubicles where the visitors would be allowed private time with prisoners. While being escorted to his relevant booth, Caesar saw all sorts of people visiting the convicted. Individuals in the area ranged from defence lawyers planning their next move or extorting money from the arrested, to fellow criminals who were attempting to sneak in some form of weapon for their arrested brethren to use within the facility.

Families visiting loved ones seemed scarce and this made for the situation to be a pitiful one.

After a slow walk and passing countless rooms, Caesar was escorted into 'Visitation Cell 178' as the sign on the door had read. The cell was a bland affair of two chairs and a table in between. He was quickly made to sit down and as soon as he did, a door on the opposite side swung open and a man in handcuffs stumbled in. The officer who had escorted Caesar to the room fastened the man in the handcuffs to his chair and then left.

Caesar now sat across a man who he could only assume to be Hideo Yoshiro. The walls reeked of despair and Caesar started to wonder as to why the man across him had killed that cop. He realized that it wasn't his place to ask that, however, and decided to get to work. Maybe this wouldn't be as easy as he expected it to be.

Hideo Yoshiro was a wreck of a man. Even though he was about six feet tall, his stoop made him come off as small and weak. Sitting, locked to a chair, the man smelled of tears and filth and Caesar wondered if this prison was really that bad. The convict across him didn't seem to have shaved in a long time and his scruffy looking hair made it quite obvious that he probably hadn't bathed in a while either.

'Mr Hideo Yoshiro,' began Caesar in a soft comforting voice, 'I'm from the Royal Citizen's Bank. I've made a deal with your brother to shift the wealth and assets of Red Sun Industries to our bank. The contract has been confirmed and your brother has already signed. Since you own fifty per cent of the company, however, your signature is also critical for this deal to go through.'

Caesar then opened that page where the man was supposed

to sign and pushed the contract across the table. He also pulled out a plastic pen that he had brought along and placed it next to the contract.

Hideo looked up and right into Caesar's eyes. A moment of uncomfortable staring passed and then the convict asked in a supernaturally cold and distant tone, 'Do you think I deserve to be here?'

Taken aback by the controversial nature of the question, Caesar fell back into his safest approach and replied with unparalleled diplomacy, 'sir, I have no right to answer that question. That would depend on one's belief in the system of laws and prison as a whole, especially the repercussions of a certain act.'

'You're just like all the others. You don't care. You just want my money.'

'Sir, it's not like that at all.'

The convict scoffed and then brought up his handcuffed wrists. Caesar watched with hope as Hideo Yoshiro picked up the plastic pen from the table and after seeing his brother's signature, signed the contract.

Twenty minutes later, Caesar was once again in the hotel car. Cigarette in hand, he let out a wide grin. It was done. Getting this account meant that he had impressed both Mulligan and the Chairman. He could now finally leave the Nakazato District and return to work, back where he belonged. And that's exactly what he did.

Boom Boom!

By adding the Red Sun Industries account to the Royal Citizen's Bank roster, it had become clear who had won the client war. Even with Brookstone's by-the-numbers approach, they had failed to even come close to what their rivals had accomplished. This glorious victory had made the people at the Head Office extremely happy and this led to a lot of bonuses being thrown around. Mulligan had scored the fattest cheque with Caesar at a close second. They were the ones who had done all the work after all.

Sitting in his office with a cigarette in his mouth, Mulligan buzzed his secretary and said, 'Send Jimmy in please.'

Minutes passed as Mulligan did nothing, but enjoy the soft deliciousness of the smoke and then there was a knock on the door. Knowing who it was already, Mulligan stubbed out his cigarette and asked them to come in.

The door opened and Jimmy strolled in, dressed in a beige suit and white shirt. It was an odd day as today Mulligan was wearing a plain dark blue suit and usually the dress code went the other way around. Jimmy took a seat and then wondered what his boss wanted to talk about. There was almost nothing important going on as everyone was in a relaxed mood after winning the client war.

Seeing the spark of curiosity in Jimmy's eye, Mulligan

reached down into his left drawer and placed his Model 625 revolver on the table. Jimmy, who couldn't have expected this in a million years, felt his face shudder with confusion.

'Relax kid. It's just a gun.' Mulligan's tone was as reassuring as ever.

'More like a hand cannon sir. I mean, look at the size of the thing. It's huge!'

Mulligan chuckled and replied, 'It is a beauty. Since we all got the bonuses, I was thinking of using mine to pick up a new piece of hardware. This revolver here is getting old and rusty. It even jammed a little the other day.'

'Jammed? Where were you using it sir? I'm pretty sure that that gun's not allowed in shooting ranges.'

'It's not. Some fool tried to mug me and the sad part was that I was the one with the bigger gun. It was truly a pitiful endeavour by the man.'

Jimmy let out a little grin. Mulligan was glad that the kid was finally relaxed.

'So listen up kid,' began Mulligan, 'I'm heading down to Roger's to pick up a new piece. I want you to come with me. It's time you started packing heat. This city isn't exactly the safest place for bankers, like you and me.'

'I don't know if I feel comfortable carrying a gun sir.'

'Look kid, it's only for your own safety. You do know how to use one right?'

'Yeah, I trained with the army for about six months.'

'Good. Then let's go.'

Both men got up and then Jimmy followed his boss through the bank and out onto the porch. The experience was different for him as his boss was attracting a lot of attention and was the subject of everyone's gaze. Mulligan, however, breezed through the crowd without a flinch and wondered how he had gotten so smooth in doing so. Experience and practice probably.

The two men waited out on the porch and moments later, Mulligan's Cadillac Sixteen pulled up. Both men got in the back and when Mulligan lit a cigarette, Jimmy followed his queue. The car ascended into motion and was soon twisting and turning through the streets of the upper city. Jimmy had heard of Roger's, but never been there before. This opportunity, even though it was during the day, seemed very exciting.

As the car moved through the streets, Jimmy broke the silence by asking a simple question, 'How come Caesar doesn't carry a weapon sir?'

Mulligan smiled at the kid and replied, 'It's cause he doesn't do street work. All he has to do is meet people in restaurants.'

The answer had been a simple one, but one that satisfied Jimmy's curiosity. The rest of the ride was as quiet as the beginning with the only sounds coming from the flipping open of a lighter to light yet another cigarette.

The car finally stopped and Mulligan led Jimmy through an alley. The kid had been expecting a much grander entrance, but he guessed that maybe that was only at night. Roger, dressed in a white suit and black shirt, stood outside the entrance and greeted the two men with a smile. Since the club didn't run during the day, Roger often catered to day clients himself.

'Mr Mulligan, how can I help you today?' Roger was as gracious as ever, but couldn't help himself from looking at the unknown kid with suspicious eyes.

Mulligan, who spotted Roger's doubt, replied casually, 'This here is Jimmy. He's my number two at the bank.'

On cue, Jimmy stretched out his hand and Roger shook it.

'So what will it be for you gentlemen today? Alcohol, cigarettes, cigars, cars, guns, suits?'

Jimmy let out a chuckle. Roger was already liked by the kid.

Mulligan smiled and replied, 'Well we need some new firepower. My Model 625 is getting old and I don't want to use my Hardballers on a daily basis.'

Roger nodded and then led the two men further down the alley and into what looked like a seemingly vacant house. As they stepped inside, two guards carrying shotguns moved aside to let the three men pass. Roger then led his two customers up a small staircase and into a room.

The room was covered with weapons on every wall. Intimidatingly enough, the range available for purchase was extremely illegal. From rocket launchers and C4 to Gatling guns and Type 100 rifles, everything was only a wad of cash away from ownership.

Eyeing the rocket launcher, Mulligan asked coyly, 'My god Roger, you could blow up a building with this thing.'

Roger chuckled and replied, 'For two hundred and fifty thousand, people can blow up whatever the hell they want.'

Jimmy, who had set his focus on a World War II MP40, asked casually, 'Isn't this gun a little old?'

Mulligan saw the idiocy in the question and replied, 'Nobody's going to walk into a gunfight with that piece of history. It's a collectible.'

Realizing that this could go on forever, Roger asked a simple question, 'So you guys are looking for handgun's right?'

Jimmy turned to the salesman and replied, 'Yeah.'

Roger then showed them a corner of the room that had eluded their eye and the two customers were in awe. Pistols and revolvers covered the entire table and wall. Some of the guns were the most futuristic ones they had ever seen.

Mulligan picked up a brown coloured pistol and asked, 'What's this?'

Roger smiled and replied, 'That's a Glock-18 machine pistol. Go ahead, fire it at the floor.'

Aiming the gun down at the floor, Mulligan pulled the trigger and was quickly greeted with extreme recoil. The gun truly was a machine pistol as it let down over ten rounds in less than a second.

'That's some powerful stuff!' exclaimed Jimmy as he saw the weapon in action.

'Too powerful,' added Mulligan.

Roger took the gun from Mulligan's hand and placed it aside. He then spoke like an educated salesman, 'I think it would be best if you went with something you're used to. Since you're used to using the Model 625, I think I have the perfect weapon for you.'

Pulling out a massive revolver, one even bigger than the Model 625, Roger handed it to Mulligan. Jimmy watched in awe.

'What on earth is this?' asked Mulligan. Even he was a little astounded.

'It's a Smith & Wesson X-Frame Model 500 revolver. It carries more of a punch than most of the other handguns in the world.' Roger replied with a proud grin.

Mulligan aimed the beast to the floor and fired. A massive hole in the floor made it clear why the weapon was regarded as the strongest, not to mention that all three men found their ears to be ringing.

'So I know what I'm buying. You picked anything out yet Jimmy?' Mulligan spoke as he continued to admire the gun.

Jimmy, who had picked out a hefty looking pistol himself, showed it to Mulligan and Roger. A quiet moment passed and then Mulligan spoke with a clear tone, 'That's a .50 Caliber Desert Eagle. You may want to go with something else. That thing takes immense practice to use properly.'

Disgruntled, Jimmy put back the weapon and continued to look around. Roger saw that the kid was lost and helped him out. Pulling out a black pistol with a small slide, Roger waved it towards Mulligan for his opinion and when he received a nod of approval, he handed the gun to Jimmy.

'What's this?' asked Jimmy unsurely.

'That's a Smith and Wesson 22A. It has a small slide and carries .22 Caliber ammunition,' replied Roger informatively.

'It looks weak.' Jimmy continued to stare at the gun with disapproval.

'Well, it is primarily a self-defence gun,' added Mulligan.

To both Roger and Mulligan's disapproval, Jimmy put down the gun and continued looking. Only a moment later, however, he picked out a gun that everyone was happy with. It was a small-to-medium sized pistol that was mostly gray-bluish in colour with black oval patches along the grip.

'What about this?' asked Jimmy hopefully as he showed Mulligan and Roger the gun.

Roger cleared his throat and replied, 'That's a Czechoslovakian CZ-G2000. It's a pretty effective pistol and one that definitely suits you.'

Jimmy then turned to Mulligan who replied coolly, 'It looks good.'

Roger handed ammo clips around and after Jimmy fired the gun a few times, he let out a sigh of satisfaction. Mulligan then paid Roger how much ever was owed and all three men walked towards the exit of the vacant house. The two guards who were carrying shotguns smiled at the three men as they stepped out into the alley and Jimmy couldn't help but wonder how much they got paid every month.

As Roger walked his clients to their car, he looked up at the sun and smiled. The weather was good today and that was a rare instance in this city. As the car got closer, Mulligan asked a simple question, 'Anything interesting going on Roger? Something that might catch my attention?'

Roger thought about it for a second and then replied, 'Well, we have a high stakes game of Top Card tonight if you want to come by.'

Mulligan let out a grin and replied, 'Top Card, huh? Yeah, I'll probably come by. What time?'

'Ten o'clock.'

The trio then reached the car and Mulligan and Jimmy got in. As soon as they were inside, Mulligan lit a cigarette and then nodded a good-bye to Roger as the car drove away. The Model 500 revolver hung heavily in his jacket and he wondered how he would balance the weight. The piece of hardware was definitely a good buy though, even though it only had a six-round clip, Mulligan knew that the firepower more than made up for it.

A couple of hours later, Mulligan sat in his office cleaning his newly purchased gun with intricate delicacy. He was using a soft handkerchief to shine the barrel and was still surprised by just how big the weapon was. Even the bullets simply reflected a sense of absolute power.

Interrupting the delicate and enjoyable procedure, the phone rang. Mulligan put down the weapon and answered the call.

'What is it?' asked Mulligan with a slightly irritated tone.

'Mr Benjamin Dover from the Brookstone Bank is waiting to talk to you,' replied the secretary calmly.

'Alright, put him through.'

There was a moment of waiting and then Mulligan heard Dover's voice echo in from the other end of the call.

'Why'd you call me Dover?'

'Listen up Mulligan, because you roped in that international client, Red Sun Factories or whatever, my bosses think that I messed up our chance to get ahead. Because of you, I'm getting demoted to unit manager at Head Office. Do you know how much shame you have brought to me?'

'You're calling to tell me all this? Why should I care?'

'You should care, no, you're going to care because my replacement is going to ruin your life just the way you ruined mine.'

'Who's your replacement?'

'Michael Hunt.'

The call ended. It was the last time that Mulligan would ever speak to Benjamin Dover. Michael Hunt, on the other hand, was a man that everybody in the banking sector had heard of over the past few years. He was supposedly a drug addict who had gone to jail a couple of times. On the other hand, however, the man was a genius manager who had saved every company he had worked with from going under. The fact that Brookstone had brought this guy in could only mean one thing: they were desperate.

Sitting back in his chair, Mulligan lit a cigarette. He didn't want to think about it, but he couldn't stop himself from wanting to. Deciding that precautions had to be taken, he picked up his phone and asked his secretary to connect him to the Chairman. After waiting on hold for fifteen minutes, his call was finally answered.

'Mulligan, I've heard things are going exceptionally well.'

'Yes, they are sir, but an issue has recently come into play.'

'What is it?'

'Well sir, Brookstone has brought in Michael Hunt as their new Head of Regional Operations.'

'Michael Hunt? I've heard of that young man. He has quite an exceptional history.'

'Yes, he does sir and keeping that in mind, I was wondering if I could ask you for something.'

'Go ahead.'

'Well sir, it would be safest for us if I could have Caesar on permanent retainer. Michael Hunt is too much of a risk to be taken lightly and having Caesar working with me would give my branch the edge it needs.'

'Caesar is one of our best Client Prioritization Executives. This is a lot you're asking for.'

'You know I have substantial reason though sir.'

'Fair enough. You can have him.'

'Thank you sir.'

The call ended. Knowing that he now had Caesar working with him permanently, things didn't feel out-of-control anymore. He stretched deeper into his seat and continued to puff away on his cigarette. A few minutes later, there were no more drags to be taken and it was stubbed out. Mulligan then got back to cleaning his magnificent gun. As he polished the smooth exterior, he fantasized about how much pleasure he would get by using that beast of a weapon to put a bullet between Michael Hunt's eyes. He hadn't even met the man and yet he already wanted to kill him.

Twenty minutes passed as Mulligan did nothing, but clean his gun and think. His thoughts dwelled upon how he should play it out with Hunt and what he should and shouldn't do. After formulating many theories in his mind, but taking none seriously, he realized that maybe brainstorming with Jimmy could help.

He buzzed his secretary and asked for the kid. Five minutes later, he was in the office.

Jimmy sat down and Mulligan lit yet another cigarette. Watching his boss smoke suddenly made him want to smoke too and twenty seconds later, he lit a cigarette in his mouth as well. As both men exhaled slowly and enjoyed their classic brands, Jimmy couldn't help but wonder if maybe the reason that he had been called to the office was to talk about his newly purchased gun.

'What's going on boss?' asked Jimmy breaking the peaceful silence.

'Something's come up.'

'Great, just when things were going smoothly. Well, I guess good things don't last forever.'

'That's what they say. Well anyway, Dover got fired.'

'You mean Benjamin Dover from Brookstone?'

'Yeah.'

'Well isn't that a good thing?'

'I thought it would be, but turns out that his replacement is quite a threat. A man named Michael Hunt. Have you heard of him?'

'Everyone's heard of Hunt boss. He's a drug-addicted management whiz.'

'Well so you know why I consider this to be a problem.'

'Don't worry too much. It'll take years for Brookstone to

even catch up to our level, no matter who they have as their manager.'

'Regardless, I want to send a message. Make it clear that we shouldn't be taken lightly.'

'You sure?'

'Yeah kid. You got any ideas?'

'Well we could poach one of their clients. It'll make them flinch for sure.'

'That sounds good. You take care of it.'

'Who should I go after?'

'It doesn't matter. Make sure that they are small-fry though.'

'I understand.'

Jimmy got up from his seat and stubbed out his only half finished cigarette. He then stepped out of his boss's office and walked back to his own. Play time was over. He now had work to do.

Half an hour later, Jimmy sat in his office still going over paperwork. His office was a medium-sized windowless unit with orange walls and bright white floors. Plastic glass shelves hung in well-selected places and all the furniture was black in colour. The table, however, was a massive contrast as it was painted bright white and was a size too large for a room of such proportions. Overall, the office gave a young and contemporary feel and that was just what Jimmy had been aiming for.

After scrolling through about twenty prospective options that ranged from drug-dealers to sandal-makers, Jimmy decided on a simple and easy target. If things went right, he could be done with this by the end of the day.

The target was an aging woman by the name of Maurice Donaldson. Currently in her early fifties, the woman was taken care of by her two loving sons and simply speaking, she didn't seem to need a bank account. One of her son's was a successful reporter while the other was a lawyer.

Taking down her address and deciding to approach her at home, Jimmy headed down to the porch and waited for the bank valet to pull up with his car; one of the perks of being a high-level employee. The valet pulled up in a custom light-green Chevrolet Camaro, a very charismatic and eye-catching automobile, and then tossed the keys to Jimmy who entered it as soon as the valet got out.

Stepping down on to the accelerator, Jimmy swerved through the roads of the upper city and even drifted when he could. Mulligan had taught him how to and he had been exceedingly grateful for learning the beautiful technique. As he drove down the roads on high-tension speeds, almost every driver of every car looked at his Camaro for at least three seconds. Even he knew that his car was a piece of art and nothing made him happier than when people stopped to appreciate it.

Twenty minutes later, the car pulled up in front of a cute yellow house that had a small front yard and sparsely placed pebbles as a path. On the left half of the yard, a large bowl lay on a stand with water in it. Every few minutes, a pigeon could be seen swooping down to enjoy a drink.

Jimmy got out of his car after making sure that he hadn't parked in an illegal spot. He then walked to the house and softly knocked on the door. When there was no response, he knocked again, but this time he heard a voice from within shouting, 'I'm coming!'

Another minute passed, but then the door finally swung open to reveal, who Jimmy could only assume to be, Mrs Maurice Donaldson. The woman was dressed in a long dress and had reading glasses hanging around her neck. She seemed old for her age, but her skin seemed to be smooth and that gave a hint of what her face may have looked like when she was young.

She smiled a loving smile and asked, 'Well how can I help you young man?'

'I'm James Wolfenstein from the Royal Citizen's Bank. My friends call me Jimmy though. Would you mind if I came in?'

The woman looked Jimmy up and down and upon judging that there was nothing to worry about, she stepped aside and let him in.

Stepping into the beautiful house, Jimmy could only imagine what a great childhood this home must have held for her sons. Soft carpeting and young furniture gave the place a very homely atmosphere and the barrage of pictures that covered the walls made it clear that the home had served a very traditional and noble purpose.

'Have a seat,' said Miss Donaldson kindly as she led Jimmy into the living room and then they both sat down.

'So how can I help you?' she asked after she got settled on a sofa.

Jimmy cleared his throat and replied, 'Well Miss Donaldson, we feel that your banking needs would be better suited with us. We have a special programme for people over forty-five, where if they want, we can deliver cash and cheques to their home. Also, we have a special helpline number, which you can call if you ever need any form of fiscal assistance.'

'But I have been with Brookstone Bank for many years. Mr Dover knows me by name.'

'Mr Dover was moved up to the Head Office recently. Miss Donaldson, we only ask you because we genuinely care for the comfort of our clients.'

'Son, since you came to personally meet all this way, I will give you my account. Brookstone has never shown me such care even though I have been with them for over two decades.'

'Thank you, Miss Donaldson.'

Getting up, Jimmy nodded a thank you and then left the lovely home. He took in the sunlight of the hot sun as he strolled the short distance between the home and his car and wondered if he would be any different if he had grown up in such a place. On the other hand, he had done his job and that should be enough to make Mulligan happy as well as to send a message to Hunt.

The next morning, Mulligan sat reading a newspaper in his office. Even though it was early in the morning, he had a cigarette in his mouth. His face, however, made it clear that he was astonished and horrified at the same time. The headline of the newspaper read, 'Home Invasion leads to 3 dead' and the rest of the article went on to detail the brutal shootings of Mrs Donaldson and her two sons.

Without knocking, Jimmy burst into the office with a pale look on his face. He had clearly read the article as well.

'What the hell happened here? She was such a nice and innocent old woman! Who would do this?' His voice portrayed the terror he felt.

'I don't know kid, but you should relax.' Mulligan tried to be as calming as ever.

Breaking the tense mood, the phone buzzed and Mulligan picked it up.

'Mr Michael Hunt from Brookstone Bank wants to talk to you sir,' announced his secretary calmly.

Mulligan was annoyed, but since he had never spoken

to the man before, he asked for the call to be put through.

'Mr Mulligan?' asked Hunt's voice in a cold tone.

'Yes, why are you calling me Hunt?'

'To make it clear that you cannot mess with me. Today's headlines reflect the repercussions for attempting to steal my clients. I do not take threats lightly.'

'You killed the old Mrs Donaldson? She wasn't even a meaningful client!'

'She betrayed me.'

'You're psychotic.'

Mulligan put down the phone before the call could continue. He didn't want to speak to Hunt anymore. Looking up, he realized that Jimmy had probably heard the whole conversation. This wasn't good.

Jimmy's face was now cold and distant. He spoke calmly, 'I am going to kill him.'

'Not so fast. He's dangerous. There's a way of doing things. I want you to take the day off and ease up. I'll take care of Hunt.' Mulligan tried to sound as reassuring as he could.

Reluctantly getting up and stepping out of the room, Jimmy felt as though a piece of him had died. Deaths had taken place because of business before, but this had just gotten too far. Killing an old lady who wasn't even in the business was simply unacceptable. It was okay to go after other members of a bank as long as you had a solid reason, but this was just an example of how twisted men like Hunt really were.

As soon as Jimmy left the room, Mulligan leaned back into his chair and exhaled deeply. Hunt had seriously messed up and now it was time for him to go. He had barely even taken over Brookstone and already he had black-marked himself. Mulligan wondered if this had happened because of the man's drug use or if this was how he had managed to help other firms survive. Maybe he had saved every firm he had worked with by killing the competition. Nothing seemed to swing in Hunt's favour right now and that only meant one thing, Mulligan was going to have to pay a visit to Don Ponzarelli.

Sitting in the Don's chamber always made Mulligan feel like he was being done a favour. The Don carried himself with such a force that he even controlled the ambience around him. Even though he was carrying a gun and the Don wasn't, Mulligan was still the one who was intimidated.

'So what have you come to speak to me about Mr Mulligan?' asked the Don with an epic tone in his voice.

Mulligan handed him the day's newspaper and pointed at the headline.

'It is a pity,' said the Don, with sympathy in his voice.

'It is cruelty. The man who killed this woman had no good reason. She was just an innocent old lady.'

'I feel there is more to the story than you are telling me.'

'The new Head of Regional Operations for Brookstone is a man named Michael Hunt. This lady was a client of his. When we got into talks with her about switching banks, he killed her.'

'I believe that there is an unwritten law against stealing clients in your business, however.'

'She approached us. We were going to decline.' Mulligan lied convincingly.

'Fair enough. So you want this Hunt man to disappear I assume?'

'Yes.'

'How soon do you want this?'

'As soon as possible. We don't want him killing anymore

people over misunderstandings.'

'You have earned my loyalty, Mr Mulligan. I will take care of this as soon the situation allows me to. Go in peace.'

Mulligan got up from his seat and then thanked the Don. Michael Hunt was soon going to be a dead man.

Hunt sat in the living room of his house, polishing his set of dual Desert Eagle pistols. He was a skinny man who almost looked anorexic because of his regular drug use. He had heavy set eyes and husky black hair that never allowed him to look professional, even when he was wearing a plain black suit like he was today. Without a tie and the top button of his white shirt hanging open, the man looked like he was going to a nightclub even though he had just returned from work.

Hunt had planned everything that he wanted to do from before he even reached the city and the murder of Miss Donaldson was necessary collateral damage. He knew that Mulligan would try and send a message and he had planned for every possibility. He had even anticipated that Mulligan would go to the Don and try to have him killed and for that reason, he sat polishing his beautiful pieces of weaponry waiting for the assassination squad to arrive.

An hour passed, then another. Just when Hunt was planning on giving up and going to sleep, a black sedan pulled up and three men got out. All of them were dressed in black suits with black ties. One of the men carried a shotgun while the other two carried pistols. Hunt couldn't tell the models because of the large distance between them.

Jumping out of his seat and checking his clips, Hunt steadied both his pistols and hid behind a nearby wall. The door was perpendicular to him and he guessed that the three men would burst through there.

Moments passed as Hunt silently waited for the three gunmen to enter. Finally the doorbell was sounded and almost instantly after, the three men in suits burst into the room and let rounds fly in every direction. They were clearly idiots hoping to hit him with a stray bullet as not even one of them fired at the wall, behind which he was hiding.

Soon the three men decided to go their separate ways and investigate the house. The fact that they hadn't seen Hunt concealed behind the wall could only be called a miracle. Hunt decided to go after the man with the shotgun first as he posed the greatest threat. He had gone upstairs and Hunt silently followed him. As soon as he was on top, Hunt found the shotgun-wielder peeking into a bedroom and decided that it was time to start the killing.

Having screwed a silencer onto both of his guns, Hunt didn't need to worry about sound and instantly let bullets loose on the man carrying a shotgun. Bullets went through the black suit and blood poured from countless wounds. The man hadn't even had a chance to aim his shotgun and already he was on the floor bleeding to death.

Hunt put in new clips and then headed down the stairs. One of the other killers was in the kitchen looking out the window when he got five rounds in his back from Hunt's Desert Eagles. His body had fallen to the floor loudly, however, and it was quite possible that the last remaining gunman had heard it.

The possibility became reality as Hunt heard shots being fired from his right. He then felt more bullets fly past him as he jumped out of the line of fire and into the kitchen. The gunman slowly approached the kitchen wondering if he had caught his target with even a single round. His question was quickly answered as Hunt jumped in front of him unwounded, and let rounds fly from his pistol. The last gunman took one to the head and three to the neck before he fell dead onto the floor.

Hunt had just taken out the last member of an entire mafia assassination squad and that meant people were coming after him; people who had the city dancing on the tip of their fingers.

Sympathy for the Devil

The boat rocked gently as Hunt lifted the last black bag off the boat and threw it in the water. He was too far out in the lake to be seen by anybody and the weights he had attached to the bottom of the bodies would ensure that the bags wouldn't come up floating anytime soon. Thinking about it now, killing those mobsters had clearly been a rash decision.

Dumping the bodies had been harder than he had guessed and upon deciding that dumping them in the river would be the safest way to go, he had bought a couple of concrete blocks and black garbage bags to get the job done. 'Sleeping with the fishes' was what the old-time gangsters had supposedly called it and Hunt was beginning to see why it was a preferred method for accomplishing this task.

The bodies, however, were only a minor problem; he had pissed off the Don and that was going to cause him serious grief. Reaching the conclusion that there was only one way of dealing with problems in this town, Hunt turned on the ignition of the boat and headed back to shore.

Facing the Don in his office, Mulligan could only hope for good news. The fact that Hunt had showed up for work today, however, was not so reassuring and even the fact that the Don himself seemed to be lost in thought didn't exactly put Mulligan's mind to rest.

After taking a deep breath and then taking a sip from the glass of water that lay in front of him, the Don spoke, choosing his words carefully, 'As I had assured you, I sent a few of my men to Mr Hunt's house.'

'He showed up for work though,' said Mulligan as he pointed out the obvious.

'I am aware of that. My men were unable to complete the job and became fatalities as Mr Hunt was already waiting for them when they arrived. Even with their experience, they had no chance overcoming an ambush.'

'An ambush by one man? That seems far-fetched.'

'It is not as simple as it sounds.'

'I understand. So what are we going to do about this?'

'Well, we are going to do nothing. I, on the other hand, will make sure that Mr Hunt gets what he deserves. I now have a personal vendetta against him.'

'He killed an old lady for god's sake.'

'I will take care of it.'

Mulligan, who was dressed in a simple beige suit and white shirt today, got up from his seat and thanked the Don. Hunt was in big trouble.

As the Cadillac Sixteen roared through the streets and headed back to the bank, Mulligan sat in the back seat with a cigarette in his mouth. He was lost in thought as he stared out at the everyday life of the city around him. Considering going after Hunt himself seemed to be the thought that popped most into his head, but after weighing the factors clearly, especially the fact that the man had dropped three professional assassins, he thought it might be best to let the Don handle it.

The cigarette finished and Mulligan threw it out of the window where it fell on sidewalk. The car continued through the winding streets of the city and as it headed onto the bridge that connected the lower and upper city over the river, he saw Hunt as he drove his boat towards the shore. Even though there was no evidence of this, there was no doubt in Mulligan's mind that the man on the boat had been dropping bodies into a massive undersea grave.

The boat reached the dock and Hunt hopped off. The name of the boat, which was imprinted on both sides and the back, was 'Treasure Hunter' with a clear emphasis on the word play. After tying the boat to the dock, Hunt headed up a small flight of stairs that led to the main road where he found his car waiting for him, just as he had left it. Since this was one of the poorer parts of the city, he was always worried that someone might try to boost his car and sell it for parts.

As Hunt got into his white Mazda RX8 and drove back towards his headquarters at Brookstone, he calculated the probability that his car was rigged to blow up and when chances indicated that it probably was, he just hoped that he was lucky today. Twenty minutes later, his car stopped in front of the bank and he quickly got out. When there was no explosion, he let out a sign of relief and returned to the safety of his office.

Carrying his Remington 870 Express Pump-Action shotgun, Santino stepped into the Don's office. He was a tall yet heavyset man dressed in a black suit and a dark green shirt that hung loose. A tie was out of the question and his heavily tanned skin well-suited his dangerous face.

'Santino, you know I call upon in you in times of dire need so there is no need for me to explain to you that the task I am going to delegate to you now is of utmost importance.' The Don's voice carried a sense of finality that made Santino feel queasy.

Taking a deep breath, Santino asked in his incredibly deep voice, 'Who is the target?'

The Don took a moment, as if to let something sink in and then said, 'Michael Hunt of Brookstone.'

Santino nodded and without any further questions, he walked out of the Don's office and left the seedy hotel. Down the block from where his boss conducted his operations, Santino approached his black Ford Explorer and got into the driver's seat. He didn't want to waste any time thinking over details and planned to get done with his target as soon as he could.

For hours, Santino sat in his car waiting for Brookstone Bank to close. He was parked just past the building in a side alley and had a clear view of the parking lot. His prime interest was in the Mazda RX8, which he had bribed one of the guards to find out was the boss's car. He checked his watch and the time indicated that there was still a good thirty minutes before closing time. Wondering what to do to pass the time, he made the simple decision of cleaning and reloading his gun once again. Doing so would ensure that his beautiful Remington would never jam up on him and never would he be in a gunfight without a gun.

Santino put in the last shell and then looked up to see employees pouring out of the bank. Closing time had arrived and it was time to get down to business. Turning the key, the ignition came on and the Ford Explorer crossed the street and entered the parking lot. Circling around leaving cars and the pedestrian crowd, Santino arrived close to the Mazda and found his target, Hunt, getting into his car. A quick well-aimed shot from the Remington suddenly rang out and instantly there was panic in the parking lot. People hurried to get out of there while the Mazda failed to move. It was hopeful to think that he had gotten his target, but since he hadn't seen Hunt take the bullet and there was no blood either, Santino fired again and then again.

The side of the Mazda facing the Remington's wrath was quickly ruined but fortunately wouldn't have to face anything more as police sirens could be heard approaching. Santino jammed on the accelerator and quickly drove out of the parking lot and then away from the scene. On his way out, he had popped out a round into the chest of the guard he had bribed for good measure. He didn't need people identifying him as the shooter.

Hunt let out a sigh of relief and rose from his crouched position as he heard the Ford Explorer depart and the police approach. He had been blessed with yet another miracle as not a single shot from the attacker, who he could only assume that the Don had sent, had scratched him. Ten minutes later though, he did find out that friendly old Bill, the guard, had taken a hit and as a result, now there was collateral damage from both sides.

After lying to the police about seeing some teenagers fire the guns, Hunt headed back to his home and decided he needed to fix things and do it fast. He had been formulating a plan in his mind and now would definitely be a good time to put it into action. Even though he didn't want to admit it, this attack had shaken him and made him realize that he needed to do more to protect himself or soon he would be knocking on heaven's door.

Standing across the Don in his office, Santino feared for his life. The Don's expression was that of grave disappointment and that only meant that the situation was bad. The last time the Don had been this disappointed with someone, a surly government agent, he had gotten axed in his home for his wife and children to see. The message had been clear that day; don't disappoint the Don.

So today, when Santino had found out that Hunt had survived and told the police that the attack had been carried out by teenagers, it would be difficult to persuade the Don to not bring out the axe man. Ten minutes had passed since Santino had entered the office and the room was overcome with such a heavy silence that both men could hear each other breathing. Unusually, Santino had also been relieved of his prized Remington before entering while usually most of the Don's men were allowed to carry their weapons when they were called upon for a meeting with the Don.

The Don, realizing that he had sweated out the other man enough, began to speak in such a powerful voice that Santino could almost physically feel the words coming out of the Don's mouth, 'When I ask you to do something Santino, I expect you to do it yourself.'

'With all due respect sir, I am quite sure that Mr Hunt is lying. I have substantial proof that it was me who went after him.'

'Prove me wrong and I will be grateful that my very own underboss isn't a weakling.'

Santino pulled out a cutout of a newspaper article related to the incident and placed it on the table for the Don to see. Moments passed as the Don carefully read through the paper and then studied the accompanying picture of the guard who was shot dead.

'I have read a similar article. Where is your evidence that you were the one who pulled the trigger?'

'The car of the attacker is said to be a black Ford Explorer, which is the car I own, and the damage to the Mazda RX8 as well the death of the guard is said to be caused by a Remington, which is the shotgun I own.'

'Fair enough. I now want to know how on earth you managed to fail a hit on a civilian. If it was a member of another family, I would have understood, but this man is just a plain banker.'

'Sir, with all due respect, if this man could drop our entire assassination squad then maybe he is more than just a banker. Mr Hunt is a dangerous man.'

The Don didn't reply and simply leaned back in his chair stroking the fabric on his left thigh. He then nodded as an indication for Santino to leave and the man quickly did. The truth was that the Don understood that his underboss had a point. Hunt was no simple civilian. He was dangerous and this is why further measures would have to be taken into account when planning the next hit.

Santino left the Don's office with a sigh of relief. He had managed to convince the Don and was glad that he had done so. If he had somehow failed, he was sure that he would soon enough find out, probably with the strike of an axe to his face. It wasn't a pleasant thought, but Santino hadn't survived in a world so dangerous by thinking pleasant thoughts.

As one of the guards at the door handed him back his Remington, Santino once again felt slightly more reassured. He was afraid of death, but having his trusty shotgun with him made him feel that maybe, just maybe, he could even put a few rounds in the Grim Reaper himself before being dropped dead.

Jimmy stood waiting outside the Royal Citizen's Bank when a Mercedes SLS pulled up and the passenger side door of the two-door car swung open as an invitation for him to get in. When he looked around unsurely he heard Caesar's familiar voice coming from the driver's seat, 'Get in kid!'

Jimmy, dressed in his classic navy-blue suit and white shirt, got into the car and smiled at the man next to him. Caesar, wearing a light blue suit and white linen shirt, sat in the driver's seat of his beloved car and after ensuring that the kid had gotten in and all the doors were closed, he put his foot down on the accelerator and the car boomed into motion.

'So this is the SLS huh?' asked Jimmy coolly as he admired the leather in the car.

'Yeah,' replied Caesar, charmingly as usual.

Quiet moments passed as Jimmy pulled out a pack of cigarettes from his pocket and lit two. He handed the first one to Caesar and put the second one in his own mouth. He then lowered the passenger side window to enjoy the fresh circulation of oxygen through the car even though it was scorchingly hot on the outside.

'Hey, you want to see something cool?' asked Caesar with a coy smile.

'Definitely,' replied Jimmy excitedly.

Caesar pressed a button under the in-built stereo. This caused a small portion behind the gearbox to open up and a small ashtray was brought up. Jimmy, being unsure if it really was an ashtray, waited for Caesar to make the first move. He was glad that the other man tapped the top of his cigarette twice and then watched the ash fall. Following Caesar, Jimmy too tapped his cigarette and dropped the extra ash that had barely hung on moments ago.

Even though Jimmy was already grinning as an indication of how much he liked this little feature, Caesar flashed him a look of wanted approval. Realizing his duty as a guest in the car, Jimmy widened his smiled and replied, 'This is amazing.'

The car ride continued quietly as the two men enjoyed their cigarettes and the ashtray. Twenty quiet minutes passed and then Caesar turned on the stereo, which played The Rolling Stones' 'Forty Licks Disk One'. Jimmy had no idea where he was being driven to but had been informed that his opinion was required on something. Since Caesar had permanently moved back to the city, he and Jimmy had become more than just colleagues who worked together and their initial work relationship had grown into a full-fledged friendship. Both men would often go out drinking together and on the occasional weekend, even clubbing.

The beautiful and elegant SLS finally pulled up and both men got out and found themselves facing a house in Park Woods. It had a wide area but the structure itself, which was centralized, was not too big. A small cement path led curving through the grass and the two men walked over it, enjoying the magnificence of the sprawling land.

The housing structure itself, a two-storey building in the centre, was extremely contemporary and much in accordance with both Jimmy's and Caesar's taste. It was painted black on the outside and had five massive windows, out of which three were on the upper floor while the other two were on either side of the entrance door. The roof was a slanting edge with one side much higher than the other and it further added to the contemporary ambience that the house exuded.

Now standing just outside the door, Jimmy asked, 'So let me guess, this is your new house?'

'You got that right.'

'So what are you going to do with all this land?'

'Well, I was thinking a nice putting area in the back, a pool to the left, a fountain in the front and a small party area on the right. Oh, and I was also thinking of putting up a neon sign that said 'Caesar's on top; one of those pink ones that blink.'

Jimmy chuckled. 'You're not serious about the sign are you?'

Caesar smiled and replied, 'Of course not.'

After studying the exterior for a few more moments, both men entered the house and looked around. The carpeting throughout was furry and black in colour. Oddly enough, Jimmy discovered, even the bathrooms were carpeted. The walls remained a consistent white throughout the house. On the ground floor, the living room was right in front of the entrance door. Further down, there was a bathroom on the right and the kitchen to the left. The kitchen was connected to a twelve-seat dining room, which opened up into the back of the open-air part of the plot.

On the top floor, still black-carpeted, the white walls seemed damp. There were four bedrooms on this floor, out of which one had been converted into a private area by Caesar. The architecture was clearly odd. The private area held a massive eighty-something-inch plasma screen television that was hooked up to a Blu-Ray DVD player. On the left wall was a massive shelf that held a humongous movie collection while on the other side of the room there were pool and billiards tables. It was the dream room for most men. The bathroom connected to the private area was quite impressive in itself as it held a hot-tub that was big enough to comfortably seat six burly men, though Caesar's neurotic sense of cleanliness probably meant that he would be the only person who would ever actually step into the hot-tub. Across the hot-tub there was another plasma screen television, only forty-something inches though, that was connected to the Blu-Ray player in the main section of the private area through wireless streaming. A truly elegant set up.

As the tour of the house finished, Jimmy sat down on a sofa and murmured, 'This is a really great house and it's going to be even better once you finish the work outside.'

'Thanks Jimmy, it means a lot to me.'

'Are you still going to buy that yacht you wanted though? I mean this must have really made a dent on your bank account.'

Caesar chuckled and replied, 'No, I'm not. I thought about it, but it doesn't make sense to own a fancy boat in a city where the only nearby water-body is the filthiest river known to man kind.'

As Jimmy drove towards his home in his Chevrolet Camaro at the end of the day, he couldn't help thinking about how fantastic Caesar's private area was. If he saved up a little, he could definitely afford something similar himself. Considering in his mind the physical areas of his home, he came to the conclusion that converting one of the bedrooms like Caesar had would be the simplest way of implementing things.

Looking forward to purchasing a massive television, hot-tub and pool table, Jimmy jammed down the accelerator on his Camaro and started drifting. A few cops saw him break about a dozen traffic rules, but they had more important work to do than chase down speed-limit offenders. As he approached an annoying gridlock and realized that he had had his fun for today, Jimmy pulled out a cigarette and lit it up. It had been difficult for him to learn how to smoke and drive at the same time, but now that he had, he could do the two things he enjoyed most at the same time.

As the black gate of his home swung open and he entered his house, passing his top-notch security system, Jimmy could feel that something was off. He slowly entered and walked towards the living room. His heart was struck with panic and he broke out in an almost instant sweat when he found Michael Hunt sitting on his suede sofa with a beer in his hand and pointing a gun at him.

'Hello Mr Wolfenstein, or do you prefer Jimmy?' asked Hunt in a cold voice.

'How the hell did you get in Hunt?!'

'Your security system isn't all that great. I disconnected the power to your home and since your automated security system takes six minutes to reboot, I had more than enough time to simply stroll in.'

'Are you here to kill me?'

'If I wanted you dead, you'd be so already.'

'So what do you want?'

'Why don't you sit down and we can talk.'

Jimmy, still slightly shaken by this unexpected sight, remembered that he was carrying the CZ-G2000 pistol that Mulligan had bought him. He couldn't take the risk of pulling it out, however, as Hunt already had the gun aimed at him, or maybe he could.

Quickly whipping out his gun and pulling the trigger, Jimmy heard nothing but a click and all Hunt did was let out a slight chuckle.

'Guess you haven't used a pistol in a while Jimmy. There's supposed to be a bullet in the chamber before you can fire,' Hunt continued in a cold and condescending tone, 'Drop the gun to the floor and then sit down. We need to talk.'

Having no other options for retaliation, Jimmy let the pistol drop from his hand and then sat down across Hunt who was still aiming a silenced Desert Eagle at him.

'So what do you want to talk about Hunt?' asked Jimmy coldly.

'Well, it seems that I have gotten off on the wrong foot with certain people, Mr Mulligan and the Don to be exact.'

'Yeah that happens when you kill innocent old ladies.'

'Watch it. I'm the man with a gun here.'

'So what do you want from me?'

'I need you to do me a favour.'

'Do I have a choice?'

'No.'

'Well, it's not a favour then, is it?'

Giving up on attempting to explain the situation to the kid, Hunt pulled out two briefcases that had been concealed from vision. They were well concealed on the side of the suede sofa that he sat on. He then placed both briefcases on the table and handed Jimmy a letter.

'What's all this?' asked Jimmy, questioning the two briefcases.

Hunt flicked open one of the cases and turned it towards Jimmy. It was filled with neatly bound cash from top to bottom.

'Cash? Who do you want me to pay?' Jimmy failed to understand the situation.

'Just take these two briefcases to Mulligan and hand him the letter. He'll know what it's about. If you don't I will have to find you and hurt you so much that your own family won't be able to recognize you.'

'It'll be done.'

'You better hope so.'

Hunt got up from the sofa and walked towards the exit of

the house. Jimmy considered loading up his CZ-G2000 pistol and going after him, but something about the briefcases that lay on the table made him do otherwise. He just sat where he was and thought about what could possibly be going on. Had Mulligan and Hunt made a deal? It was impossible to know. Jimmy considered reading the sealed letter, but maybe Mulligan would know that he did so and he would get into trouble. It was best to just obey instructions and get the briefcases to his boss.

The next morning, Mulligan sat in his office with a cigarette in his mouth. He had turned towards his window and was enjoying the view of the city below. It was a magnificent metropolis that had the perfect conditions for criminals to thrive in and gangsters to get richer. All of that black money meant that money laundering ran rampant and the best way to get clean money was to go through a bank.

The phone buzzed and Mulligan quickly spun around and picked it up.

'Sir, Jimmy is here to see you,' announced the secretary in a cool voice.

'Send him in,' replied Mulligan as he took another drag from his cigarette.

Jimmy, dressed in a black suit and black tie, strolled into the office and placed two heavy briefcases on the table. He then handed Mulligan the letter that Hunt had given. He was looking pale and he felt uncomfortable.

'Hunt came to my house last night.' Jimmy sounded distant.

Mulligan, who was still trying to understand what all was on his table, quickly turned his attention to the pale young man across him, 'Michael Hunt?'

'Yes. I walked in to find him waiting in my living room.

He then gave me all of this at gunpoint and asked me to deliver it to you.'

Mulligan, quickly realizing that the kid wasn't used to all this, asked sympathetically, 'You okay, kid?'

'I'll be fine. I'm going to take the day off today.' Jimmy then strolled out of the room.

A silent moment passed as Mulligan considered the situation. He then opened the letter that Jimmy had given him. It was a simple handwritten note, which had a deep message.

This is my gift to you. I hope we can let bygones be bygones.

Curiously wondering what the 'gift' was, Mulligan opened both briefcases to find just what he was expecting; a lot of cash. After spending two hours counting the money, the total sum came up to five hundred thousand with two hundred and fifty thousand in each briefcase. Deciding that this money was meant for the bank and not for himself personally, Mulligan buzzed his secretary.

A moment later, the door swung open and the secretary entered his office. She was surprised by the massive amount of cash on the table, but quickly concealed her emotion.

'This here is five hundred thousand. Please put it in the administration fund.' Mulligan spoke in an innocent voice so as to not raise suspicion about where the money was coming from.

The secretary simply nodded in response and after spending a few minutes replacing the money in the briefcase, she exited the room carrying one case in each arm. Mulligan was glad that Hunt had sought to pay reparations. In this city, money could buy anything and in this case, it had bought

Hunt a chance to live life without constantly having to worry about retaliation from Mulligan. This, however, only solved half the problem.

Hunt strolled into The Fisherman's Loft, Don Ponzarelli's headquarters, carrying two briefcases full of money, similar to those he had given Mulligan. He knew there was a seventy per cent chance that he would be shot on sight, but this was a risk he was willing to take.

As he entered the filthy old hotel, he barely took in the surroundings before he was smacked on the back of the head with one end of a shotgun. Almost instantly blacking out, Hunt knew that it was probably not the smartest idea to stroll in here without an appointment.

Twenty minutes later, Hunt jerked awake when he felt a splash of cold water on his face. He was sitting in the Don's office with Santino aiming a gun right at the back of his head. The Don sat across him with an angered look on his face and the two briefcases of money he had brought with him lay open on the table between them.

Minutes passed and Hunt didn't dare say a word. Having a Remington shotgun pointed at the back of your head was an extremely intimidating situation. The Don, who seemed quite ferocious, broke the silence.

'You do know that we are the ones who have been after your life Mr Hunt?'

'Yes.' Hunt spoke in a calm tone.

'So then why would you walk in here, knowing that we will end your life?'

'I come in peace.'

'That's the only reason you're still alive. If you were carrying even a nail-cutter, you would not be breathing right now.'

'That is what I want to change. I believe that we got off on the wrong foot and I have come here to make amends. There is two hundred and fifty thousand in each of those two briefcases and I believe that should be enough to repair our relationship.'

'What makes you think I won't take the money and still have Santino here put a bullet through your head?'

'Because Don Ponzarelli, I believe that you are an honorable man.'

Back Door Man

Over the past few weeks, things had once again become calm in the city. Hunt had made a good decision by buying his safety. No one, not even the Don, would hold a grudge against someone who gifted them half a million in cash. Mulligan still ensured that The Royal Citizen's Bank maintained a big lead against Brookstone. Jimmy was getting closer to buying his Lexus. Caesar had finished all the renovations on his home. So, when Mulligan was being driven to the Rising Sun restaurant in his Cadillac Sixteen, he didn't think about what all could go wrong at this meeting, but simply enjoyed his cigarette instead.

It had been a short eight-minute drive from the office to Mulligan's favourite restaurant. The Rising Sun was located on an important juncture and therefore, occupied a prime location. On one hand, it was situated next to the bridge that led from the upper city to the lower city and on the other hand, it was located on one of the biggest roads in the entire district.

After getting out of the car and taking a deep breath of fresh air, Mulligan let his cigarette drop to the floor and slip into the gutter. He then slowly walked to the entrance of the restaurant, which looked like a simple red building with windows on the outside, and was greeted by the maître d' with a big smile.

'Mr Mulligan, it is good to see you again!' said the maître d' in his heavy mid-European accent.

'You too, Gustav. I'm here to meet someone.' Mulligan was much less enthusiastic.

'Yes, Mr Richard Cross. He is already here.'

Gustav, the maître d', then led Mulligan through the restaurant. Walking through the restaurant, Mulligan had to meet several people and shake a lot of hands. The prime location and impressive décor of the restaurant meant that many politicians and businessmen also used this as a place to discuss work and since Mulligan was a banker, he knew mostly all of them.

Usually it would take Gustav about thirty seconds to lead a client to his table. With Mr Mulligan, however, it seemed to take forever. The man seemed to know everybody in the restaurant. Fortunately for him, he was a big spender, otherwise this annoyance would have led to him being treated like everyone else and that would mean just directed to a table, not exactly led there.

The Rising Sun, as the name may already hint, was the best restaurant for Japanese food in town. It had blood-red carpeting and the walls were covered with paintings by Japanese artists. The ceiling was slanted towards the middle, like the inside of a house with a snow roof, and was primarily decorated with oak wood. The waiters were dressed in white shirts and white coats with a black bow tie. This was matched to the rest of the décor with red pants and black shoes. Gustav, on the other hand, wore a completely white suit with a red shirt in order to differentiate himself from the waiters.

Mulligan, wearing a black suit with a black shirt, approached his table-for-two. The person he had come to meet, Mr Richard

Cross, was already seated. Cross was a scrawny yet tall man dressed in a beige suit and white shirt. He had clean cut hair and was wearing expensive snakeskin black shoes on his feet.

Sitting down and studying the man across him, Mulligan asked, 'Do you mind if I smoke?'

Cross made a gesture with his hand and replied accordingly, 'Feel free.'

Lighting a cigarette and taking a few drags, Mulligan thanked god that this restaurant allowed smoking indoors. He then looked at Cross and clearly asked, 'So do you know why I'm meeting with you today, Mr Cross?'

Looking down in shame, Cross answered, 'Because I begged you too.'

'Why did you beg me to come here Mr Cross? What is so important that we couldn't talk about it on the phone?'

'I'm in an urgent and desperate situation.'

'I deal with people in urgent and desperate situations every single day. Tell me, what is important about yours?'

'My son was in an accident. He's dying and I don't have the necessary medical insurance to cover the operation. That's why I need an urgent loan.'

'It'll take at least two days to draw up the contract. Why are you coming to me? Why don't you go to a health insurance firm and see what they can do?'

'I did. They said that the only thing I could do was apply for an urgent loan.'

Something didn't feel right to Mulligan. He decided to get down to business, 'What would the value of the loan be?'

'Two hundred thousand dollars.'

'Two hundred thousand dollars? What kind of an operation is this?'

'One that will the save the life of my child.'

'I'll tell you what Mr Cross. You come to my office tomorrow morning and I will have the loan papers ready.'

'I need the money in cash.'

'Why?'

Cross paused and then replied, 'A cheque may take too long to process.'

'Alright fine.'

'Thank you.' Cross got up and was about to leave when Mulligan stopped him and asked, 'What's your son's name?'

There was a long pause and then Cross replied, 'Tim.'

'And what hospital is he at?'

Mulligan patiently waited as there was another long pause.

'Grand Central Hospital,' answered Cross.

Then before Mulligan could say anything else, the man quickly headed out of the restaurant. Something was not right. Cross could easily be lying and that's why it would be best to check if his son really was in hospital before doling out any amount of money.

After Cross left, Gustav approached Mulligan and asked, 'So you'll be eating alone today, I suppose?'

Mulligan nodded in response and then gave his order of food. Enjoying a variety of sushi with favourites being eel and salmon, he lit a cigarette and sipped the glass of red wine he had ordered. It had been a while since he had eaten at this restaurant and he wanted to enjoy every moment of this while he had the chance to.

As soon as Cross walked out of the restaurant, he let out a massive sigh of relief. He truly believed that Mulligan had fallen for his story. He then got into the backseat of a red Mercedes SUV where he was surrounded by three thugs. One was driving, the other sat in the front passenger seat while the third sat next to him.

The leader seemed to be the one driving and he barked at Cross, 'Did that banker believe you?'

'Yeah, he did. I gave him the sob story about my son as we had planned. He says he's going to give me the money tomorrow morning.' Cross spoke with his voice trembling in fear.

'You better hope so,' replied the lead thug, 'you have a lot of gambling debts to repay and if you don't come with the money in three days, Roger said that you're going to be a dead man.'

Cross was then thrown out of the car by the thug who had been sitting next to him in the backseat. He fell out onto the curb where his head hit a trashcan. Moments later, he began to sit up and then watched the Mercedes SUV drive off.

After lunch, a glass of wine and then a couple of shots of sake, Mulligan asked for the bill. It was brought to him within a couple of minutes and turned out to be steeper than he had expected, probably because of the alcohol he had ordered. After paying with his platinum card, he got up from his seat and walked out of the restaurant. Without saying anything to anyone, his car was brought around and he got into the back seat. It was about four o'clock in the afternoon and with the heavy heat setting in, the whole city seemed to be getting drowsy.

'Back to the office boss?' asked the driver looking at his boss's sleepy state.

'No, I need to go Grand Central Hospital.' Mulligan decided to check up on the Cross kid before he forgot about it.

'Emergency?' asked the driver.

'No.'

Mulligan then slid back into his seat and lit a cigarette. Outside he watched the city pass by and it was surprising when he saw that there were almost no pedestrians out on the street. The heat seemed to have a great effect on everyone.

The drive to Grand Central Hospital was about thirty minutes long and Mulligan dozed off for about the last fifteen minutes of the journey. When the car did finally pull up in front of the entrance, he jerked awake and stepped outside. The weather seemed to be cooler now and was a great relief to those who planned to step outside.

Grand Central Hospital was the oldest of the trio of hospitals in the city. It was also the only one that ran a major non-profit programme for healthcare, under the age of twenty-five, and that made Cross's story even more unbelievable. On the outside, the structure of the building seemed to be made out of a variety of blocks. The main tower was a tall rectangular structure in the middle. The other wings seemed to be added towards the outside and had almost fortified the main tower with shorter block-shaped structures on all sides.

The building was mainly coloured white, but had a lot of large windows. The main tower in the centre, however, seemed especially bland as it was an object of plain white with the only windows being on the top floor. Truly an odd looking structure if observed by itself. The block that Mulligan now faced had an open-air ground floor that was dominated mostly by pillars. It served more like the entrance to the parking garage than to a hospital. A massive fiberglass blue sign at the top of the block read, 'Medical' while the signs on the other buildings read, 'Surgery', 'Emergency', 'GCH Initiative' and 'Administrative' respectively. The 'Administrative' building was the main tower while the 'GCH Initiative' was the non-profit wing run by the hospital.

Lighting a cigarette and walking into the main 'Medical' wing, Mulligan was instantly greeted with stern looks from the hospital personnel. One of the guards then approached him and made the matter clear, 'No smoking. It's a hospital.'

After nodding in return as an indication that he had understood the issue, Mulligan stubbed out his cigarette and then threw it in the trash. He then approached what looked to be a reception area and addressed the woman behind the counter, 'Good afternoon.'

The woman flashed him a snarky look and replied, 'Three of my patients died from infection right now so it's not really a "good" afternoon.'

Mulligan, who felt as though he had made some sort of a mistake, replied softly, 'I apologize.'

The woman retorted with a comforting smile and said, 'It's okay. What do you need?'

Mulligan took a deep breath and decided to get down to business, 'I'm looking for someone. He's a young male, last name Cross. He seems to be in need of a two hundred thousand-dollar operation.'

'Did you just say two hundred thousand dollar operation?'

'Yes.'

'Well even if there were such an expensive operation taking place, I'll need proof that you're family before giving out that information.'

Reaching into his wallet, Mulligan pulled out a hundred dollar bill and then handed it to the woman who accepted it casually and slipped it into her pocket.

'So can you help me now?' asked Mulligan calmly.

'Sure,' replied the woman. She then coolly searched her computer for the information and about forty-five seconds later, she looked up and replied, 'There's no such patient here. I even checked the surgery wing since you said he needed an operation. No one named Cross is admitted in the entire hospital.'

Nodding a thank you, Mulligan exited the building and as soon as he stepped outside, lit a cigarette. Moments later his car appeared in front of him and he got into the back seat. Deciding that the weather was too good to ignore, he rolled down the window and enjoyed the wind striking his face at harsh speeds. As the car left the hospital compound, the driver turned around as though he was waiting for instructions. Mulligan told him to get back to the office and returned to enjoying the wind on his face and the nicotine in his lungs.

The fact that there was no patient named Cross in the hospital meant that Richard Cross had lied about his son needing an operation. Such an extravagant lie indicated that he was desperate and everyone knew that desperation of that depth could only come from having your life on the line. Lying to Mulligan hadn't been a good idea and now when Cross would come to visit him for the loan tomorrow morning, he was going to get what he deserved.

An hour later, Mulligan sat in his office going over some files with immense focus. They were detailed information packets on the most recent client acquisitions by Brookstone and all of it indicated the fact that Hunt really knew what he was doing. Under his command, the lead between Brookstone and the Royal Citizen's Bank had already started reducing at a steady rate, but there was still nothing to worry about. RCB was still way ahead. Mulligan, however, as a precaution, always read about any new client gains made by Brookstone as it was safest to keep tabs on what the enemy was doing.

As he closed the file on the latest client, his phone buzzed and he quickly answered it, 'What is it?'

'Caesar is here to see you sir.' The secretary's tone was professional as usual.

Wondering what was going on, Mulligan replied, 'Send him in.'

The door swung open and Caesar, dressed in a beige suit and pink shirt, entered with a charming smile on his face. He then sat down across Mulligan and simultaneously, both of them lit cigarettes. A short moment passed as they enjoyed the first drags of their cigarettes and then Caesar spoke in his usually charming tone, 'I was wondering if you're free tonight?'

'Maybe, why?' Mulligan answered safely.

'Well, the renovations on my house just finished. New pool, fountain, putting green and the works so I'm having a party today to, well, officially showcase my new home.'

'Well, I'll definitely come by. What's the address?'

'Park Woods. It's the third house on the right if you enter from the east gate.'

'You know, I live in East Park Woods too?' added Mulligan to Caesar's surprise.

'Really?'

'Yes.'

'Well, that's interesting.'

Caesar then stubbed out his cigarette and got up to leave. As he walked out the door, Mulligan could only wonder as to whether he would attend the party or not. Even though he considered Caesar to be a friend, he knew that the crowd at the event would be filled with business people and that would mean that his work day wasn't going to end until the party would end.

Deciding that he needed more information before he made a decision, he buzzed his secretary who instantly answered in an efficient voice as usual, 'Yes sir?'

Mulligan took a breath and replied, 'I need Jimmy.'

The secretary addressed the common request without thinking twice and replied, 'He'll be here in five minutes.'

Five slow minutes passed as Mulligan finished his cigarette and then lit another one. Looking out the window, the weather seemed to have become damp and the building that earlier was pleasant white now seemed to be bathed in gray.

There was a knock on the door and then Jimmy entered the office. He sat down across his boss and upon checking his pockets, found out that he had run out of cigarettes.

'Boss, can I bum a cigarette?'

Mulligan smiled and then opened his bottom right drawer. The drawer was filled with neatly stacked cigarette packs all the way up to the top. He picked one out and threw it to Jimmy who looked at him with thankful, but confused eyes. The kid wasn't sure as to if he was supposed to keep the entire pack or only take a single cigarette and return it.

Being a generous man, Mulligan smiled and said, 'Keep the pack kid. It'll be shame if you ran out.'

Jimmy smiled at the gesture and then lit a cigarette. As he took the first drag, he exhaled heavily and then slid back into his seat with the absolution of relaxation flowing through his blood.

'So what's going on?' asked Jimmy after a while.

Mulligan smiled, almost felt embarrassed, but then controlled himself and asked, 'So you're obviously going to Caesar's party right?'

Jimmy let out a knowing grin and replied, 'Of course. I organized most of it.'

Now a little confused, Mulligan asked, 'Organized?'

Realizing that his boss clearly didn't know about the relationship dynamic between him and Caesar, Jimmy answered coolly, 'Well we've become friends ever since he moved back to the city and since he was still getting adjusted, I did him a favour and helped him organize the party.'

'Oh, alright. So you can answer a question for me then?' Mulligan spoke carefully.

'Sure,' replied Jimmy with an innocent grin on his face.

'What's the crowd going to be like?' Mulligan attempted to conceal the real reason as to why he had asked the question.

Jimmy took a breath and searched his thoughts. He took a while to come up with an answer and then replied calmly, 'From what I remember, it's the usual political crowd. Caesar's quite well connected.'

'Thanks kid.' Mulligan leaned back in his chair, hiding his disappointment. He wanted to go to the party but knowing that he was going to have to work the room as soon he walked in, he had lost incentive. Since Caesar had made the effort to ask him personally, however, he knew he had to obey social decorum and at least show his face if not stay there for the entire duration.

Six hours later, the Cadillac Sixteen pulled up in front of Caesar's house and Mulligan got out from the back seat. He walked through the open gate and entered a magnificent and sprawling open area with a medium-sized house in the middle. While Mulligan had gone ahead and built as much as he could on his given land, Caesar seemed to have taken advantage of the large area to focus on the outside.

Dressed in a plain black suit with a bright pink shirt and brown leather shoes, Mulligan walked passed a grand fountain and headed towards a large area on the right, which seemed to have been designed for parties. As he approached, he realized that he recognized and knew every face he could see and that meant a lot of hands had to be shaken and a lot of fake laughs had to be laughed.

Even though he spotted Caesar in the distance, Mulligan had to go through the ordeal of meeting everyone on the way before he could reach his target. After shaking hands with a couple of investors and then a middle-eastern oil prince, he was fortunate enough to grab a cold beer from the other end of the bar before being whisked back into the crowd. This time it was the mayor, a few members of the golf club and a few valuable contacts in the public sector.

After fighting through the crowd for another thirty minutes, Mulligan finally stood face to face across Caesar and greeted him with a smile.

'Glad you could come,' said Caesar, as he smiled with genuine emotion.

'This is a great home. Very tailored.' Mulligan spoke loud enough to be coherent over the Carlos Santana song playing in the background through the speakers.

Realizing that it was time to get back to the hell of formal socializing, both men turned away and began going through the motions once again. Mulligan then decided that he could focus on more pleasant things while facing this travesty of social decorum and so he began to concentrate on remembering the name of the song that was playing.

Starting off with an extended version of 'Oye Como Va', the soft Latin Rock works of Santana then shifted to 'Evil

Ways', which if Mulligan managed to keep track of correctly, was played four times back-to-back. Then there was 'Corazon Espinado', which was followed by a cover of 'She's Not Here' and finally a version of 'Black Magic Woman' that he didn't seem to have heard before.

The shaking of hands finally ended and Mulligan went ahead and settled himself into a chair away from the bar. He then watched the other people work the crowd and tried to figure out a way to go through the motions faster himself. A waiter approached him carrying an array of drinks and he quickly picked out the plainest looking ones and gulped them down. Alcohol was alcohol and he was going to need a lot of it to get through this party.

Deciding there was nothing better to do, Mulligan got up from his seat and walked to the putting green towards the back of the house. He had spotted it a little earlier and this fantastic concept attracted him. He reached the little piece of well-cultivated grass and upon counting five holes, he picked up five balls and a putter from a green rack that stood on the edge.

Heading to one end of the green and aligning the five balls in a straight line with about five centimeters between them, Mulligan started studying the green. The bend of the grass, the slope of the ground, everything was critical if he hoped to successfully accomplish his task. After spending a few minutes studying the environment, he got down to it and started putting the balls in the holes. It was an impressive sight as one by one, each ball entered a different hole. It was almost as though he had completed some form of supernatural circuit. Smiling about the fact that he still had the ability to do this, he put the putter back in the rack all the while maintaining a cocky grin on his face.

Unexpectedly, he saw two men approaching him, but because of the dark light, he couldn't tell who they were. As they came closer, their features became clearer and he recognized one of them as Caesar. The other man he had never seen before.

'Boss, I want you to meet someone,' said Caesar in his usual charming tone.

'I'm Lance Lapidus,' announced the unknown man. Now that he was close, it was easier for Mulligan to study him.

Mr Lapidus was a big, but not tall man. He had wide shoulders and a large abdomen, but his innocent face encouraged friendliness, not hostility. He smiled a sharp grin, much like Caesar's, and was currently dressed in a plain black suit and loose white shirt. Thinking about it now, Mulligan was sure that he had definitely heard the man's name before.

After studying the man, Mulligan introduced himself in a humble tone, 'I'm William Mulligan. Head of Regional Operations for the Royal Citizen's Bank.'

Grinning, Lapidus replied, 'I know who you are Mr Mulligan. Everybody in this town does. I, on the other hand, used to work for Black Light Enterprises as a Situation Management Executive until recently, when the firm shut down.'

Suddenly, Mulligan remembered the man. He was one of the best Situation Management Executives in the country. The title was unusually fancy as what Lance Lapidus really specialized in was contacts. His entire job revolved around knowing the right people to get things done. He was an invaluable asset and Mulligan quickly realized why Caesar had brought this man to him.

Phrasing his words carefully, Mulligan said, 'Mr Lapidus, you have quite a reputation as I recall. Why don't you come work for me? I need men with contacts like yours on a daily basis.'

Lapidus, who hadn't been expecting such a straight forward approach, replied unsurely, 'I have an offer from Brookstone as well. Mr Michael Hunt contacted me the day my firm shut down. You, on the other hand, sir, couldn't even remember who I was until moments ago.'

Realizing that he had hurt the man's pride, Mulligan did the only thing he could to ensure that Lapidus didn't defect to Brookstone, 'I'll pay you thirty per cent more than whatever Hunt's offering you. I do, however, expect to see you in my office tomorrow morning at ten.'

Letting out a massive grin as an acceptance of the offer, Lapidus nodded a thank you and walked away.

The next morning, Mulligan sat smoking in his office waiting for the watch to strike ten. He had been awaiting this meeting with Lapidus as he wanted to measure the extent of the man's influence. The clock struck the eventful hour and almost instantly the phone buzzed.

'Mr Lance Lapidus is here to see you, sir.' The secretary maintained acute efficiency as always.

'Send him in,' replied Mulligan and then put the phone down.

Lapidus, dressed in a beige suit and white shirt, entered the office and sat down across Mulligan. As he saw that his boss was smoking, he pulled out a cigarette himself and lit it up.

'So I assume you want to see what kind of reach I really carry?' asked Lapidus. He was much smarter than Mulligan had anticipated.

'Yes. I need you to find out everything you can about a man named Richard Cross.' Mulligan spoke in a clear tone.

'Give me ten minutes,' said Lapidus and then got up and left the room.

As he waited for his latest employee to return with his research, Mulligan stubbed out his current cigarette and lit up another one. This cigarette, however, seemed to have crumpled with nicotine spilling everywhere and was instantly thrown into the trash. The gaping need for nicotine and tobacco wasn't going to be unquenched though, so another cigarette quickly found its way into his mouth.

As he inhaled the calming effect of his cigarette, there was a knock on the door, which was followed by Lapidus re-entering the room.

'I have everything you need,' said Lapidus as he sat down across his boss.

Mulligan, who had been expecting some form of file or folder, was surprised when he was presented with none.

'So you communicate all the information to me orally?' Mulligan voiced his doubt.

'Yes,' replied Lapidus.

'So what did you find out?' It was time to get down to business and it would be best if Mulligan actually heard what the man had to offer before bringing down the verdict on his usefulness.

'Well, Richard Cross is a consultant working in the computer manufacturing industry. He has a serious gambling problem and has been arrested thrice for petty theft. He was also arrested once last week as he tried to bribe a hospital official into opening a fake file in the name of Timothy Cross. He lives near the river on the lower side and drives a second-hand black SUV.'

Mulligan was impressed. It had taken Lapidus less than ten minutes to make phone calls and find out all of this information. He was clearly a very worthy asset.

'Thank you, Lance. You clearly know what you're doing.' Mulligan spoke in a clear and honest tone.

Lapidus, who was glad that he had impressed his boss, got up from his seat and nodded a thank you. He then left the office, leaving Mulligan once again in wait. This time for the meeting he had fixed with Richard Cross.

Minutes passed, then an hour. Mulligan was beginning to doubt if Cross would actually come. Cross had clearly attempted to scam him into a cash loan. He would then use the money to pay off gambling debts. Even to try such a thing made him feel as though he was being disrespected and disrespect was something that he despised.

The phone finally buzzed.

Mulligan picked it up to hear his secretary's voice, 'Mr Richard Cross is here to see you.'

'Send him in,' replied Mulligan and then waited as the door swung open and Cross entered the room.

Being greeted almost instantly with a cold stare, Cross sat down across Mulligan with a dead look on his face. Without saying anything, Mulligan used one hand to grab Cross's arm and hold it down. He then used his other hand to pull the cigarette out of his mouth and stub it out against Cross's bare flesh. Cross screamed in agony as he felt his skin burn and scorch.

The flame burned out and Mulligan released the man. Cross winced in pain as he covered his small burn with his palm.

'What the hell?' Cross asked in a pained voice.

Mulligan smiled an evil smile and replied, 'You try to make a fool out of me? You think I'll give you two hundred thousand in cash without checking to see if you really had a son or not?'

Cross continued to crumble in pain and replied weakly, 'I do have a son!'

Mulligan scoffed at the lie and pulled out his lighter. He flicked it open as a warning to Cross and then said, 'Don't lie to me. You needed the cash to pay off gambling debts.'

A quiet moment passed.

The pain on Cross's arm seemed to have died out and he jumped up from his seat. He then reached into his coat and was about to pull out a pistol when Mulligan saw the danger and ducked under his table. Cross fired a few randomly aimed rounds and then screamed, 'Give me the money!'

Behind the crazed Cross, the door swung open and Jimmy, who had heard the gunshots, entered pointing his CZ-G2000 pistol straight ahead. He then fired five rounds, which hit Cross right in his spine and the man dropped dead to the floor.

Guessing that the danger had been taken care of, Mulligan got out from behind the table and looked around. Upon seeing the dead man on the floor and Jimmy standing over him with a pistol, he let out a smile and said graciously, 'Thanks kid. I owe you one.'

An hour later, Jimmy and Mulligan sat in a police interrogation room being questioned about the shooting. A gruff looking officer banged down on the table and asked them, 'How did this happen?'

Mulligan let out a smile and replied calmly, 'The idiot tried to rob us.'

Money for Nothing

Lapidus, Jimmy and Caesar sat facing Mulligan in his office. All of them smoked cigarettes and oddly enough, Jimmy and Lapidus had taken up menthols. There was no particularly important business to take care of right now and all the four men were doing was using each other as an excuse for a meeting, which only served the purpose of allowing these men to enjoy their uniquely artistic blends of nicotine and tobacco undisturbed.

Five minutes passed and as their cigarettes ran out, a new batch was lit. One ashtray didn't seem to be enough to accommodate the rapid outflow of ash and, therefore, Lapidus volunteered to get one. He was still new at the bank and even though he was well-liked in Mulligan's inner circle of associates, who were borderline friends, he felt as though he needed to go the extra mile to continue to impress these people.

Getting up from the exquisitely comfortable guest chairs in Mulligan's office, Lapidus stood dressed in a black suit with a dark blue shirt and took another drag from his cigarette. He then exited the office and strolled down the welcoming and homely corridors of the bank greeting anyone and everyone who passed him by. Maintaining a friendly attitude had been the first step to attaining his unparalleled network of connections.

Continuing to smoke in the corridor and walk towards his office, Lapidus looked out through the corridor windows and stared adoringly at the sun. It was truly a beautiful city, but he never forgot the fact that this was the rich upper side and he currently moved through a well air-conditioned corridor, which was in stark contrast with the amplified heat of the crippling outside weather.

Finally, reaching his office and pushing through a plain black door with a sign on it reading F. Lapidus, he entered and grabbed the lighter that lay on his hand-carved oak table. He then emptied out the ash in the ashtray by dumping it in the trash can and wondered as to why he simply hadn't done the same at Mulligan's office. His mind quickly remembered, however, that some smokers liked to maintain their ash as a form of record-keeping to show off their superior nicotine-addiction. It was a truly odd thing to do, but no way in hell was he going to question the ways or maybe even the traditions of this bank.

Returning towards the smoker-filled office, he was surprised when he found Mulligan standing outside looking right at him. Flashing a look of confusion, he hopefully prompted an explanatory response from his boss. He got none as he drew closer but when he was within range for a whisper, he was greeted in a simple and cool tone, 'Lose the ashtray Lapidus. We have work to do.'

Following instructions like a loyal and efficient subordinate, Lapidus put aside the ashtray on a nearby table and then attempted to keep up pace with his boss as he followed him through the still-confusing architecture of the building. Minutes later, however, he found himself on the porch waiting for his boss's car to arrive.

The black Cadillac Sixteen, the elegant piece of animalistic machinery that it was, roared onto the porch and one of the employees held open the back door of the car as his boss got in and then he followed into the back seat. The door shut with a smooth bend and the car growled once again. Moments later, it was on the road heading towards an unknown destination that only Mulligan was privy to. Lapidus simply waited quietly hoping that when the time came, the job that would be given to him would be within the scope of his abilities.

As seconds passed and then excruciatingly long, silent minutes, Lapidus was still hopelessly uninformed as to where they were headed. He had heard from the rest of the staff that it would be best not to break silence when alone with the boss and he planned to follow that advice even if it meant that he wanted to claw his lungs out in frustration.

The driver found an open patch of straight road and could be seen smiling in the rear-view mirror. The accelerator was jammed down and the car picked up speed at a fiercely fast rate as it headed down the road. In the distance, a sharp corner could be seen approaching and it seemed quite clear that until and unless the driver slowed down, everyone in the car was going to face death surrounded and pierced by flame and metal.

Lapidus took a breath as the corner was way too close to avoid, but was fortunately surprised when the driver executed a perfect power-slide across two-lanes of the empty road. The front two wheels maintained a constant turned angle while the back wheels skidded sideways. It was inexplicably smooth and the success of the endeavour could be seen reflected in the driver's wide grin.

Breaking the peaceful silence, Mulligan addressed his driver and said, 'That was beautiful.'

He clearly seemed to be commenting on the driver's advanced vehicle maneuverability. The driver nodded a thankyou that was seen through the rear-view mirror and the silence returned one again. Lapidus couldn't help wonder why nothing had been said to him yet, but he could only hope that maybe it was because the task they were heading towards was so miniscule and unimportant, that it didn't need any prior planning.

Another quiet ten minutes passed as the car continued to move at a speed that was quite unsafe. The changes in the surroundings were now becoming quite prominent as they were driving passed barren empty land. This wasn't the lower city. It wasn't a part of the city at all. They had driven out of the region and seemed to be heading to a distant nowhere on the horizon.

Using every ounce of will that he could scrounge up, Lapidus still maintained oral silence.

The mood suddenly turned grim. The car turned onto the side and was now off the road. The driver picked up speed and then suddenly braked. Stopping with a jerk, Lapidus was extremely confused about the situation. It got worse, however, as he felt a large piece of metal smack him on the side of the head. The car door was then opened and he found himself being dragged out of the car and thrown onto the ground. Mulligan had gotten out from the other side and now stood over him with a large metal gun in his hand.

'What the hell is going on?' Lapidus asked as he wiped the blood gushing from the wound on his head.

Mulligan didn't say anything, but simply wiped the top of the gun and then aimed it at Lapidus's head.

'What the hell boss?' screamed Lapidus once again. He feared for his life.

'Do you work for Brookstone?' Mulligan spoke in a contained voice as he continued to aim the gun at the man on the ground.

'What? No! Of course not!' This was the last thing that Lapidus was expecting.

'Do you work for Michael Hunt?' asked Mulligan again.

'I do not! Can you put away the gun? Then we can talk about this. You clearly have some bad information.' Lapidus was almost begging.

'Are you a mole in my bank attempting to sell protected information for money?' Mulligan was still excruciatingly calm. That scared Lapidus more than the gun.

'No! No! No!' Lapidus was screaming louder than necessary.

Oddly enough, Mulligan believed him this time and holstered the gun. He then helped him up to his feet and they both got back in the car.

With both men now sitting in awkward silence, the car returned to the main road and headed back to the city. The driver once again gunned the accelerator and then turned and asked his boss, 'Back to the office?'

Mulligan answered casually, 'Yeah.'

Back at the Royal Citizen's Bank, Jimmy and Caesar sat across each other still smoking. They enjoyed the calm days when they could because the rest of the year, they were in an endless race for clients. Appreciating the little things was something that they had come to enjoy.

Jimmy stubbed out his finished cigarette and with a smile asked, 'So, do you think Lapidus survived the boss's psychotic test?'

Caesar chuckled and replied, 'Mulligan does it because he feels he has to. There is almost no way of successfully detecting a mole in the organization, but at least this way, he gets to wave around his gun and play gangster.'

Jimmy finished lighting another cigarette and then said between drags, 'Boss really does love playing gangster, doesn't he?'

Letting a silent moment pass, Caesar asked thoughtfully, 'Speaking of gangsters, didn't Hunt drop three of Don Ponzarelli's top men?'

Jimmy was surprised that Caesar had heard about that and replied, 'Yeah. He had to pay big money for his mistake though.'

'How much?' asked Caesar almost instantly.

Jimmy remembered the amount and then answered, 'About half a big-six to the Don.'

Caesar was surprised by the amount and replied, 'Nothing comes cheap in this town, does it?'

Meanwhile, the Cadillac Sixteen continued to head back towards the bank. Since Mulligan's little test twenty minutes ago, neither man had said a single word to each other. Mulligan simply hoped that Lapidus would understand the need for the incident like everyone before him had, while Lapidus simply assumed that his boss had lost his mind and had succumbed to paranoia.

'You're not the first one.' Mulligan spoke with a cool calmness.

Lapidus looked at his boss with amplified confusion and then asked, 'What do you mean?'

Mulligan looked out of the window at the city passing by and replied, 'Well, the test. You're not the first one who gave it.'

Astounded, Lapidus murmured a question, 'This was a test? What kind of sick tests do you guys take?'

'Well, about five years ago,' began Mulligan, 'the Chairman told all the regional heads that precautions had to be taken to ensure against a mole in the upper tiers of the organization. Some decided to take polygraphs while others tried private detectives. I, on the other hand, decided that this was the easiest and most effective way of doing things.'

Oddly enough, things didn't seem that insane anymore and Lapidus replied in a cautious tone, 'I guess it makes sense now that you've explained it. Nice gun by the way. What is that? The Model 625?'

Mulligan let out a sharp and proud smile. He then replied, 'No, it's bigger. The X-Frame Model 500.'

A moment passed and then Mulligan pulled out his gun and handed it to Lapidus. Observing it and estimating the firepower, Lapidus was clearly impressed by this piece of exquisite weaponry. He then handed it back to his boss and asked, 'Can I smoke in the car?'

The question was automatically answered when Mulligan lit a cigarette for himself. Lapidus followed cue and both men enjoyed their smokes as the car roared through the streets and approached its destination at lethal speeds. The test had somehow established new-found trust between the two men. Mulligan had felt this happen before and always assumed that it was because of the absolutely extreme nature of the situation.

Later that day, Lapidus sat at a corner table in the Hard Heart. Even though it was nowhere near to being the best table in the restaurant, it was preferred by him as he didn't like being centralized and surrounded by tables on all other sides. This way, he was granted a much needed illusion of privacy.

Across him sat Jonathan Pym. Pym was a skinny and weak-faced man, but had an odd aura about him. He was one of those people who were experts in their field, but didn't know how to sell their abilities to possible employers. Dressed in a black suit with a black shirt, which was an odd combination for the middle of the afternoon, Pym took another drag from a lit cigarette in his hand and then said, 'How long has it been now? A year maybe since I last met you?'

'Yeah that sounds about right. You know I honestly believe that I deserve more visits from you. We were like best college roommates.' Lapidus spoke as he took a sip from a glass of ice-water in front of him.

'Well, I'm going to be in town for a while so it won't be a problem. So you're working with The Royal Citizen's Bank now? Is it better than working at Black Light?'

'It has its moments. This bank has a very relaxed and calm way of functioning. It's almost pleasant. So what are you doing in town?'

'Picked up a contract as a Financial Consultant. I'm working with Ribera Construction. They're building a new dam on the river for the city.'

'That's a big project. Who are you banking with?'

'Brookstone, the deal was already signed by the time I joined in. You know I would have pushed towards your bank, otherwise. Honestly, I don't know if I trust Michael Hunt. You probably know him. He's the regional head.'

'Loosely. So what kind of revenue are you guys looking at over the years?'

'I don't know. It's impossible to calculate. We have nothing to worry about though; a hydroelectric dam is as good as mining gold in such a technologically advanced city.'

Lapidus didn't say anything. He was lost in thought and passed the time lighting up a cigarette. The information he had just received made Brookstone extremely dangerous. They wouldn't have any problem taking the lead with a hydroelectric dam under their belt. Even though this weighed down heavily on his moral side, Lapidus knew that he had to do whatever he could to swing this dam project in the Royal Citizen's Bank's favour. Even if it meant that his oldest college friend may lose his job.

Taking a breath, Lapidus began digging for useful information, 'So Ribera Construction, I've never heard of that firm. Is it new?'

Pym, who had ordered a dish of spring rolls as an appetizer, popped one in his mouth and then replied, 'Well, it is new. From what I can tell from the books though, it's just a massive money laundering organization. It's owned by a Cuban man named Antonio Ribera, who apparently made his fortune importing and selling cocaine.'

'Doesn't that make him dangerous?'

'Well, he doesn't know much about business so he relies mostly on hired people to do his job. It could be a problem if someone found where his money is coming from though.'

'What about the City Planning and Zoning Commission?'

'They have nothing to do with this. We only have to deal with the Commission for Heat, Power and Water.'

Having attained more than enough information, Lapidus decided that it was critical to inform his boss of his discoveries. Thanking his friend for lunch and heading outside, he signaled to the valet to bring his car around. Seconds passed and then minutes. This seemed to be the worst valet service in the country.

Lapidus's impatience, however, finally washed away when he saw his car turn the corner and pull up in front of him.

The metallic black Aston Martin Rapide was an elegant and fine-tuned machine that excited the owner every time he got into the driver's seat.

As the car sped down the city, Lapidus's amazing ability to perfectly handle the vehicle made him feel as though the vehicle had become one with the road. It was an indescribable sensation that somehow made even the closest things feel distant.

Finally arriving at the bank, Lapidus hurriedly got out and threw his keys at the valet. He then raced through the bank and minutes later, found himself panting outside Mulligan's office. The secretary looked at him as though he was crazy and the fact that he smiled a dangerous smile in return didn't help the cause.

'I need to see the boss.' Lapidus spoke clearly over his heavy breathing.

'Alright, let me buzz you in.' The secretary then followed the usual procedure after which Lapidus was given the go-ahead and he entered the office and settled comfortably in a chair across his boss.

Lighting a cigarette before saying anything, Lapidus watched Mulligan stare out at the horizon and wondered what his boss was thinking about. Finally inhaling the lovely yet dangerously toxic fumes, he spoke in a clear tone, 'Boss, we have a problem.'

Suddenly Mulligan focused his attention and stubbed out his cigarette. He asked simply, 'What's going on?'

'Sir, I was at lunch with a friend of mine right now who told me that he's acting as the financial consultant for a new dam being built on the river.'

'So what's the problem?'

'The development firm, Ribera Construction and the

Commission for Heat, Power and Water have chosen Brookstone for banking. Since it's a hydroelectric dam, everyone's going to make big money and that may even go as far as to bump Brookstone into the lead.'

'Damn it. Just when things were beginning to get simple.'

'So what's our in?'

'I don't think we have one sir. Contracts are all signed. Building starts next month.'

'There's always an in. We just need to figure it out. I can't let Hunt win.'

'We could bribe someone on the Commission.'

'No, that won't work. No one has the authority to change banks alone.'

'I know that. I meant to shut down the project. That way at least we can still maintain the lead.'

'Good thinking. We should still consider ways to swing this in our favour though. There has to be a way to take advantage of this.'

Silence took over the room as both men leaned back in their chairs with cigarettes in hand. It was critical to deal with the situation before construction began, as after that it would be impossible to do anything. Lapidus could only think of candidates for effective bribes while Mulligan estimated the possible profitability if the project was purchased from Ribera Construction. As the minutes passed, they both realized that it would be impossible to take over the project and the best solution would be to simply put a halt to it. Even to do that, however, different approaches would need to be weighed and the best one would then be selected.

On the other end of town, Pym drove his white Audi A8 at a slow speed. It had been difficult for him to get a good handle on driving and, therefore, he never experimented past an undefined safe zone. As he navigated through the streets, countless cars cut him off and overtook him, but his pride was unharmed, as for him, it was a big deal just to be behind the driver's seat. Purchasing expensive cars had further helped him cope with his lack of motor skills as they were much smoother and often simpler to drive.

The car reached its destination and turned into a lavish villa. Two guards waited on the outside of a tall black gate and had pushed it open when they recognized the incoming car. Inside a narrow road led to the main porch, which had a large waterfall in the centre. The villa itself was a massive white design with palm trees everywhere and lush greenery acting as a backdrop for beautiful scenery. The setup conveyed such an enlightened sense of relaxation that anybody who ever entered the property felt as though the beach was somewhere nearby.

Pym waited in his car just outside the entrance to the house. He watched closely as the door swung open and a man that he knew as Antony Ribera stepped out. The Cuban was wearing a black pinstripe suit with a loose white shirt that was open at the top to reveal thick chest hair. He had tousled hair that created a youngish charm and in his mouth he had a fat cigar. He wore a ring on his left index finger and openly carried a black .9mm Beretta that was tucked behind his belt.

He approached the car and indicated with his finger for Pym to get out.

'We're going to go in my car.' The Cuban spoke in an extremely heavy accent and then lead the way to the garage. Pym followed him closely through the magnificent home while relishing the simple ambience. The only thing that seemed out of place were the legions of guards who, dressed in light beige suits and white shirts, patrolled the estate carrying Mac-10s and .38 Snub Nose revolvers.

Finally, arriving at the epic garage filled with vintage cars, the Cuban continued to lead the way and both men finally stood in front of a convertible and light blue 2002 Lincoln Continental. It was a beautiful vehicle that further added to the already oceanic vibe that Pym had felt since he had entered the estate.

The Cuban took a drag from his cigar and then jumped into the front seat and Pym got in next to him. The car revved alive and Pym was honestly surprised when he saw the top speed on the tachometer was at 300 kmph.

As he saw Pym admire the vehicle, the Cuban smiled coolly and then said, 'Say hello to my little friend,' as he pulled out an M-16 with an under-barrel grenade launcher from below the seat.

'What do you need that for?' asked Pym as he jumped up in surprise after seeing the army-issue assault rifle.

'It's better to be safe than sorry,' replied the Cuban suavely and then turned on the stereo. 'Push it to the Limit' by Paul Engemann started playing. The car was then driven out of the villa and moved quickly through the wide roads of the upper city. All this while, Pym couldn't help but stare at a small globe that hung from the rear-view mirror. It was golden in colour with red text around the middle reading 'The World is Yours'.

The men rode in silence as the car pulsated with music. Many people eyed the retro vehicle as they passed it by and Pym guessed that the Cuban probably cherished the attention. As his cigar ran out and he lit another one, the Cuban enjoyed the powerful breeze on his face and the scalding heat of the sun against his forehead. Not many people enjoyed high temperatures as much as he did.

Ten minutes later, the car pulled up and both men got out. They were standing on the edge of the river looking at the fish who tried to swim upstream.

The Cuban took a slow drag from his cigar and then threw the rest of it into the water.

Pym waited a few warm moments and then asked, 'Mr Ribera, why are we here?'

Smiling at the other man, the Cuban spoke coolly, 'This is the site for the dam. I wanted you to see the physical place as to where the great structure will be built. Understand Mr Pym, this is my last resort to get out of the drug business. I am sick of playing games with my enemies and looking over my shoulder everywhere I go. This is my only chance to be able to sleep in peace once again.'

A few days later, Mulligan sat in his office with Lapidus across him. Both men sat with cigarettes hanging out from the edges of their mouths and neither of them had said anything for the past few moments.

Breaking the silence, Mulligan asked, 'It's getting bloody hot, isn't it?'

Lapidus took a drag from his cigarette and replied, 'Tell me about it. The weatherman said we hit 47 yesterday.'

Another few silent moments passed and Mulligan stubbed out his cigarette in a fashion that implied that it was time to get down to business.

'So who are we bribing?' Mulligan asked casually.

'Well there's only one person who can actually permanently shut down the project. Stewart Donner. He's the top councilman on the Commission for Heat, Power and Water.' Lapidus spoke between drags.

'Have we gotten in touch with him?' asked Mulligan inquisitively.

Lapidus looked around as though he was dodging the question and then stubbed out his cigarette. He then met eyes with his boss and answered, 'Not yet. He shouldn't be tough to swing though. You could go down to the Commission today and talk to him.'

Mulligan thought about it and then moved onto the next step, 'How much should we give him?'

Once again Lapidus seemed unsure and then answered, 'Well, it's steep. I spoke to some of my other associates who have dealt with him and in a case like this; I think it would take about a fifth of a big-six.'

'Two hundred thousand?' asked Mulligan just to make sure he had heard right.

Lapidus simply nodded in return.

An hour later, Mulligan was in the back seat of his Cadillac Sixteen with a briefcase containing two hundred thousand dollars in cash. His driver had been instructed to head to the Commission for Heat, Power and Water and was, therefore, speedily dodging traffic as the car moved towards its destination on the east side of the upper city.

Ten minutes later, the car pulled up in front of the ugly brown building that was the headquarters for the Commission and Mulligan got out of the car. He stood with the briefcase in one hand while skillfully using the other to light a cigarette. He then strolled over bad ceramic tiles and oddly placed grills towards the entrance of the building, which was nothing but a large revolving glass door. Why revolving doors were even used anymore was something that he would never understand.

Entering the lobby, Mulligan approached a receptionist

who didn't even look at him as he stood in front of her waiting to catch her attention.

'Miss, I'm looking for the office of Mr Donner.' Mulligan spoke in monotone.

The receptionist looked him up and down and then said, 'It's down the corridor, second room to the right.'

Mulligan nodded a thank you and began to walk away, but was quickly stopped by the receptionist calling out to him, 'Wait!'

Mulligan reluctantly turned around and once again faced the woman. 'What is it?'

The secretary spoke coolly, 'Mr Donner may be in a meeting.'

Mulligan scoffed and replied, 'I doubt it.'

'Well I have to check anyway.' The woman then started going through what looked like a decade old register. Minutes passed and then she looked up as though she had finished.

'Well?' Mulligan was annoyed.

'He's not in a meeting. Go right ahead.' The woman spoke with pride, which annoyed Mulligan even more. He then walked towards the office stepping over ugly white marble flooring and facing damp brown walls. Upon arriving at the door, he saw an imprint reading 'Mr S. Donner. Head of Local Commission.' The imprint was right in the centre of the door with the rest of it being cheap wood.

Mulligan knocked on the door and was asked to come in. Upon entering he saw a small office with two ugly wooden chairs for visitors, a metal table and a leather chair for Donner. It was truly a hideous sight with the best part being the window that looked out onto the parking lot.

Steward Donner, on the other hand, was a short stocky

man who was bald and had large glasses. He was wearing a black suit with a red tie and maintained an arrogant expression on his face. What he had to be arrogant for was something Mulligan couldn't even guess. Realizing that small talk was unnecessary, both men got right down to business.

'I'm William Mulligan, regional head for the Royal Citizen's Bank.'

'Sit down Mr Mulligan.' Donner had a very rowdy voice.

'I'm here about the dam project.'

'The contract's already been signed with Brookstone. I can't help you there.'

Mulligan put the briefcase on the table and opened it up. He watched Donner's eyes shine greedily as he saw the money.

'What can I do for you, Mr Mulligan? That sort of money can buy you a lot of services.'

Mulligan smiled at the idiocy of the man and said, 'Shut down the entire project and you can have the two hundred thousand in this briefcase.'

Without thinking, Donner grabbed the briefcase and placed it on his lap. He then spoke childishly, 'As long as I'm alive, no dam will ever be built on that filthy river without your permission.'

Mulligan chuckled at how easy the deal had been and then left the building. As he was getting into the back of his car, he simply hoped that the cancellation of the project wouldn't be traced back to him as that could lead to a lot of problems. After all, this would be enough to have both Michael Hunt and the Cuban drug lord coming after him.

Gimme Shelter

Antonio Ribera, the Cuban, sat across Hunt in his office. The mood was excessively grim as they had just heard about the cancellation of the dam project. The fact that Pym was also supposed to be a part of this meeting and hadn't yet arrived only further added to their agitation.

Pym sat behind the steering wheel of his Audi A8. The car was parked in the Brookstone parking lot, but he didn't have the courage to enter the building. He had heard about what had happened and was angry at how naïve he had been in giving Lapidus all that valuable information. He could have made a lot of money, but now, he would consider himself lucky if the Cuban and Hunt failed to figure out what had happened. After summoning courage based on countless false reassurances, he got out of the car and entered the building.

Walking slowly through the bank, dodging the eye contact, Pym felt like a man without a country. He had no one to rely on, no one to turn to in such turbulent times. As he drew closer to the office, he could feel the fear of mortality course through his veins. It was highly possible that Hunt had figured out what had happened and if so, there was no telling as to what they would do to him. Losing the chance to make millions can drive the noblest of people to do evil and the two men that he was about to face, were far from noble.

There was a knock on the door and then Pym entered. Without looking anyone in the eye, he settled into a seat next to the Cuban and as the silence continued, he lit a cigarette. He took a few drags, still looking at the floor and came off almost instantly as a man who had something to hide.

'What the hell's wrong with you?' barked the Cuban, 'Sit up straight. You're acting like a child.'

Pym followed the directive and then looked at the two men. Hunt was lost in deep thought and was staring out the window. His clenched fist, however, made it clear that he wasn't happy. The Cuban, on the other hand, was just annoyed—he hadn't actually lost much money, but that didn't matter to him. It was the loss of the chance to make a lot more money that frustrated him.

'So does anybody have any idea as to how this happened?' Pym asked calmly. He was beginning to regain confidence as he saw that the other two men were clueless about what had happened.

'I think we need to pick up some people and find out what went wrong.' The Cuban spoke as he lit a cigar. He was dressed in a light-blue suit and white shirt today that somehow made him look even more dangerous than when he was dressed in black. It probably had something to do with his mental volatility.

Hunt scoffed and retorted, 'We are not going to go around kidnapping random people. This is a bank, not a cartel.'

The Cuban ignored the remark and continued to enjoy his smoke. He leaned back in his chair and looked up at the ceiling, studying the slowly revolving fan. He didn't have much experience in the legitimate business world, but could feel that he had been sabotaged in some way.

Pym stubbed out his cigarette on an ashtray on the table and then asked Hunt, 'So what reason did the Commission give?' He had been informed that the project had been cancelled through a phone call and, therefore, the details still evaded him.

Hunt pulled out a crumpled piece of paper from his drawer and tossed it onto the table. It had probably been crushed in his hand out of anger. Pym was afraid of even imagining what the banker would have been like when he had gotten the news.

The paper contained the usual bureaucratic information with the main cause for project cancellation given at the bottom as 'Unrequired Resource'.

Pym was taken aback by the oddness of what he had read and asked, 'Unrequired Resource? What does that mean?'

Hunt pulled the paper back towards him and once again crumpled it in his fist before throwing it into the trash. He then answered the question, 'It means that the city already has enough electricity and, therefore, there would be no social benefits of building the dam.'

'Something doesn't fit right. I can feel that someone has intentionally disrupted our plans.' The Cuban added. His accent seemed to get heavier when he talked and smoked at the same time.

They were beginning to catch on and Pym was starting to get worried again. He would have had no idea as to how any of this had happened until and unless he had received that call in the morning. Lapidus had phoned him and told him that he had been feeling very guilty. When Pym had asked why, Lapidus had explained to him how he had sabotaged the dam project by giving his boss some vital information. He had even offered to get him a decent job. Pym had been skeptical at first as he hadn't heard anything about the cancellation, but all of that instantly died away when he received a call from Hunt telling him that the city had shut down the project and asked him to come in for a meeting.

Controlling his fear and continuing to maintain a straight face, Pym lit another cigarette and once again studied the other two men. Hunt was still lost in thought, probably trying to figure out what had happened and how it could be rectified, while the Cuban was still leaning back in his chair with a cigar in his mouth and blankly staring at the fan.

'I think we should go talk to this Stewart Donner. He's the one who issued the order after all.' Hunt spoke calmly.

The Cuban looked at Pym and then back at Hunt to answer, 'I don't think he had anything to do with it. He was probably just used to putting the cancellation into action. I feel, from personal experience, that this comes from your rival. They were the ones who benefitted the most from this anyway.'

They were catching on and this weakened Pym.

Hunt thought about it and then said, 'You're right. It probably was Mulligan and his men. No one else had motive. We should do something about this. Find a way to confirm our doubts.'

Acting recklessly, Pym became defensive. 'I think you're wrong. This was probably one of the other construction firms, not the bank. For example, a company like Armor Benedict Construction has a lot more to gain from this cancellation than the Royal Citizen's Bank does.'

The Cuban stubbed out his cigar and said, 'You're right Pym. It could be a construction firm as well. There's only one way to know for sure though, we need to talk to Stewart Donner. He can tell us who bribed him.'

Hunt nodded in agreement. He was beginning to feel more confident about catching the culprit. Realizing this, Pym quickly got out of his chair and without saying anything, he left the room. It was an odd thing to do, but Hunt and the Cuban were more focused on other things to notice that right now.

As soon as he was outside Hunt's office, Pym pulled out his phone and dialled for Lapidus. Seven long rings later, the call was answered.

'Lance Lapidus here.'

'It's me. There's a problem.' Pym tried not to sound weak.

'What happened?' Lapidus knew that what he was about to hear couldn't possibly be good news.

'I'm with Hunt and the Cuban. They're going to go after Steward Donner, the guy from the Commission of Heat, Power and Water. They know that he's the one who was bribed and they plan to find out who bribed him.' Pym had spoken swiftly.

'I'll take care of it.' Lapidus then hung up.

Pym returned to Hunt's office with a neutral look on his face. He was going to try and create as much doubt as he could to ensure delay in going after Donner. The Cuban watched closely as Pym sat down and then asked him, 'Where were you?'

Taking a breath, Pym lied professionally, 'I had to cancel a meeting.'

Back at the Royal Citizen's Bank, Mulligan heard an urgent knock on his door, which was followed by Lapidus entering. Seeing the worried expression on the other man's face, Mulligan knew that something bad had happened and in light of recent events, it was probably something to do with the dam project.

'Talk to me,' said Mulligan calmly.

Lapidus took a breath and replied, 'They're going after

Donner soon. If they talk to him they'll find out that we had bribed him and got the project shut down.'

'How do you know this?' Mulligan wanted to ensure that the information was good before reacting.

'My friend Jonathan Pym; he's the one who gave us the information about the project in the first place. He's in a meeting with Hunt and the Cuban right now.'

'The Cuban?' Mulligan hadn't been expecting such an odd way to refer to a man.

'Antonio Ribera of Ribera Construction. He was the contractor for the dam.'

Mulligan didn't need to know anything else. He opened his first drawer and pulled out his gargantuan Model 500 revolver. After loading it with hollow-point ammunition, he holstered it in his jacket and then led the way through the bank and out onto the porch with Lapidus following him closely.

After getting into the back seat of his Cadillac Sixteen, Mulligan said to Lapidus, 'Follow me in your own car. We might need it.'

Obeying orders, Lapidus jogged to his nearby parked Aston Martin Rapide and jumped in behind the wheel. He then followed the Cadillac Sixteen through the roads of the upper city and even though he was in a sports car, he found it hard to keep up with the Mulligan's sedan.

In the back seat of his car with a cigarette in his mouth, Mulligan had almost no idea as to what he was going to do once he got to his destination. Was he going to put a bullet in Stewart Donner's head to shut him up forever? Was he going to give him extra cash and tell him to leave the country? Or was he going to find Hunt and the Cuban already waiting for him with an army? The first two seemed like the preferred scenarios. The third just felt deadly.

Ten minutes later, both cars pulled up in front of the ugly Commission building. After parking, Mulligan and Lapidus stood outside on the porch studying the environment. Nothing hostile seemed to be lurking around.

'Are you carrying a weapon?' asked Mulligan as he continued to look around. He was dressed in a black suit like everyone else and that helped him blend in.

'Yeah, a Colt Anaconda. It's a .44 Magnum.' Lapidus was beginning to get a little anxious.

'Good. Now I want you to go in and get Donner. I'll keep an eye out here.' Mulligan spoke as he casually placed his arm in his coat, ready to draw his gun. It didn't seem suspicious until and unless one knew what he concealed within his jacket.

Lapidus headed into the building and approached the receptionist. She was as arrogant as she had been with Mulligan and didn't even look at the man who stood waiting for her attention.

'Miss, I need to see Mr Donner.' Lapidus spoke commandingly yet politely.

The receptionist rolled her eyes and then checked her register. Silent moments passed as she went through the list of people who signed in today. During this time, Lapidus could do nothing, but looked around to study the environment. That's when he noticed another problem; there were security cameras all over the place. His train of thought was interrupted when the receptionist looked right at him and said, 'Mr Donner is not in office today.'

Nodding a thank you, Lapidus turned around and quickly left the building. As he stood outside, he realized that Mulligan was not where he had left him. After looking around, he found him standing next to a tree a little distance away. It was a strategic location as it didn't attract attention while at the same time all the cars could be seen long before they turned towards the porch of the building.

Lapidus approached his boss, who as usual, stood with a lit cigarette in his mouth. Mulligan saw the other man drawing closer and asked, 'Where's Donner?'

'He didn't show up for work today.' Lapidus answered calmly.

'He must be enjoying his bribe money. Okay, here's what we're going to do. I'm going to get in my car and head out while you go back into the Commission and get me his address. I'll have to go visit him at home.' Mulligan spoke as he stubbed out his cigarette.

'We have another problem though. There are security cameras inside. If they get their hands on them, they'll see you walking into the building with a money bag.' Lapidus knew that there was very little chance that Hunt would actually retrieve the footage, but this was a chance that he wasn't willing to take.

'Take care of that as well then. The address first though. That's more important.' Mulligan got into his car as soon as he finished speaking.

After watching the Cadillac Sixteen drive away, Lapidus headed back into the building. He knew that he was going to have to be very careful when accomplishing his task, even the smallest mistake could have him thrown in jail.

As he entered through the revolving doors and once again stood in front of the rude receptionist, she flashed him a look of annoyance and asked, 'What is it?'

Lapidus pulled out a hundred dollar note from his pocket and placed it slyly on the table. He watched as the receptionist quickly pocketed it with a smile on her face and then asked, 'I need you to do me a favour. Tell me where I can get Mr Donner's home address.'

The receptionist looked surprised upon hearing the odd request and pointed the way to the Human Resources office. The hundred-dollar bribe hadn't been necessary, but it was enough to ensure that she would keep her mouth shut if Hunt and the Cuban came around asking questions.

Following directions, Lapidus headed towards the Human Resources office and was surprised by how ugly the interior of the building really was. It was almost as though no one had even bothered to try and make things look attractive. It was by far the laziest workplace one could ever see.

Approaching a heavy wooden door with a sign reading 'H.R.' on it, Lapidus knocked and then entered. It turned out to be a ridiculously small office, as Mulligan had noticed with Donner's, which had almost no effort made towards making it more comfortable.

The woman who sat behind the desk was probably about thirty-five years old and was dressed in shabby clothes and had dirty hair. She seemed to be under severe work stress and why someone would work so hard in the public sector was something that Lapidus would never understand.

The woman flashed a look upwards and then asked, 'What do you need?' She had a perpetually annoyed tone much like the receptionist.

Lapidus smiled, in hopes of being charming, and asked, 'I need Mr Donner's home address.'

Suddenly, the woman stopped working and with all her attention, looked up at the man standing across her. She took a deep breath and then said, 'I'm afraid I can't give you the information without proper authorization.'

A lazy way to get a bribe, but one that Lapidus could see through easily. 'How much will this authorization cost me?'

The woman studied Lapidus for a few moments as she attempted to figure out how much money she could extort the man for. He was dressed in an expensive and tailored gray suit with a black shirt. He was a big man, but still well-groomed with an almost perfectly shaved face. Everything pointed to the fact that this man was clearly loaded and could be milked for a lot of cash.

'Ten thousand.' The woman declared it an absolute fashion.

Lapidus let out a little and chuckle and asked, 'You think I'm going to pay ten thousand dollars for an address? Who do you think I am?'

The woman smiled in an evil way and answered, 'To me, you're Mr Moneybags. Now, I know you really want this information and I know ten thousand won't even scratch your bank account. So let's see the money.'

Lapidus considered pulling out his gun and shooting her in the head. He considered it seriously. He hated ignorant people like the woman he faced right now. Killing her, however, would obviously make things much more difficult than needed so he decided to act sane and negotiate.

'Being realistic,' Lapidus began, 'I'll give you five hundred dollars for the address.'

The woman, for some unknown reason, chuckled and then said, 'You drive a hard bargain. I'll give you my best price, nine thousand nine hundred and ninety nine dollars.'

Lapidus clenched his fist. He was beginning to get angry. 'You think this is funny?'

Realizing that she was pushing the man too much, the

woman decided to act rational and said, 'Two thousand dollars.'

'One thousand. That's it.' Lapidus had a sense of epic finality in his voice.

The woman agreed and then went through her files. As she searched for the address, Lapidus pulled out a thousand dollars in cash from his wallet and placed it on the table. Minutes passed and the woman finally found the file she was looking for. Opening it to the first page, she copied down the address onto a piece of paper and handed it to Lapidus. As the address was studied by the man opposite her, the woman picked up the cash from the table and counted it. She had just made easy money.

Lapidus stepped out of the office and dialled for Mulligan. Almost instantly, his call was answered.

'Do you have the address?' Mulligan asked anxiously.

'18 Wolf Lane.' Lapidus wondered if the address was correct. He had never heard of Wolf Lane.

'Alright. I know where that is. I'll take care of Donner and meet you back at the office. Make sure to erase the security footage.' Mulligan then hung up.

Lapidus slipped his phone back into his pocket and then tore up the piece of paper containing the address. His main job was done. Since he hadn't seen any 'No-Smoking' signs within the building, he lit up a cigarette and walked around looking for the security room.

He considered asking someone where it was, but that was a question that instantly raised suspicion. He would have to find it on his own, even if it meant that he had to roam around helplessly in this ugly government building.

As he sat in the back seat of the white Mazda RX8, Pym feared for his life. Hunt was driving with the Cuban sitting next to him and unfortunately enough, their destination was the Commission for Heat, Power and Water. Pym had done all he could to delay this inevitable car ride and he deeply hoped that he bought enough time for Lapidus and his boss to take care of things.

The Cuban, who had a fat cigar in his mouth, was calm and contained as always. Pym had come to deeply respect this fact about the man and assumed that this profound sense of always being relaxed was derived from the fact that the man didn't care much about the situation. A conspiracy to get a project shut down was probably child's play to a man who had grown up running drugs and carrying out assassinations.

Lapidus had been roaming around for quite some time now and had made it onto the first floor. The ground level was mostly offices with the only other rooms being a large hall and a pantry for coffee, tea and biscuits. The first floor, however, held more promise as it had larger and more administration-based rooms that indicated that the security room, in all probability, was on this floor.

As he continued to stroll calmly through the ugly and dingy halls, Lapidus was surprised when he felt a tap on the shoulder and saw a short man looking at him aggressively. The short man was dressed in a badly-fitting black suit and white shirt. He seemed angry and asked, 'What the hell are you doing?'

Lapidus, who hadn't been expecting this sort of hostility, replied, 'What's it to you? I can be here. This is a free and public area.'

The man scoffed and said, 'I don't care about that. Stub out your cigarette. You can't smoke here.' He then turned around and walked away.

Feeling stupid for misunderstanding the man, Lapidus let his cigarette drop from his mouth onto the already filthy floor and stubbed it out under his shoe. He then continued roaming through the halls looking for anything that even remotely looked like a security room.

As he got closer to finishing his round of the floor, he saw a blue room with a glass pane in the centre. There was no sign saying it was the security room, but from the way it was designed, it seemed like it. Moving closer for a better look, he spotted two security guards sitting inside the room staring at countless video screens. They seemed sleepy and Lapidus didn't blame them because it was quite obvious that things of security interest rarely ever happened in this building.

Deciding on a straight forward approach, Lapidus checked his wallet for cash and found that he had two thousand dollars left. That would be more than enough to take care of these two lazy men. Knocking on the door, Lapidus waited for it to be opened. After the passing of a minute, he realized that maybe these two men actually were asleep and wondered if maybe he should sneak in and erase the tapes himself. Realizing that he didn't know much about security cameras, however, he decided that it would be better to pay for the service and this time he knocked louder. Hearing the sound, one security guard jerked awake and grumpily approached the door and opened it. Sleepily he asked, 'Who are you?'

Lapidus smiled and said, 'Wake your friend up and then we'll talk.'

Realizing that the man meant business, the guard did as he was told and returned to the room where he shook the other guard awake. Both men sleepily staggered toward Lapidus who greeted them with a knowing smile.

'I have a deal for you both.' Lapidus spoke coolly.

'What kind of deal?' asked the security guard who had been the second to awake from sleep.

'I'll give you two a hundred dollars each if you delete yesterday's footage.' Lapidus acted as though it was no big deal in order to make the two guards feel more comfortable. When he saw that they were feeling unsure, he added, 'Come on. It's easy money.'

One of the guards, who realized that the man with the money was right, went back into the security room and returned with a collection of disks. He then handed them to Lapidus who in return handed each of them a hundred dollars. It had been cheaper than he had expected. These two hadn't even bothered to bargain.

As he put the disks in his coat pocket, Lapidus asked, 'There are no backups or anything right?'

One of the security guards shook his head and then went back to sleeping. Lapidus then turned away from the security room and began to trace his steps back to the lobby. He wondered if he should call Mulligan and inform him that he had the footage, but realized that it wasn't necessary. His boss was probably more focused on dealing with Donner anyway.

As he entered the lobby once again, Lapidus was taken aback by what he saw. The situation was clearly not what he was expecting. Hunt and Pym stood with another man heatedly questioning the receptionist. Pym seemed slightly distracted while Hunt seemed frustrated. The third man, dressed in a light-blue suit with a cigar in his mouth, seemed powerfully foreign and that's when Lapidus realized that the man was probably Antonio Ribera, the Cuban.

Walking quickly, Lapidus did everything he could do to

ensure that the trio of men wouldn't see him and he felt safer when he got through the revolving doors and was out of the lobby. He then swiftly jogged towards his Aston Martin and placed the footage disks in front of his top left wheel. He then got into his car and drove away from the building. He had felt a slight bump when his car had rolled over and crushed the footage disks and he hoped that no broken edge had punctured his tire. After driving for about seven minutes, he realized that there was nothing to worry about. There were no cars following him, the disks were destroyed and his tires were fine.

As the Cadillac Sixteen roared towards the home of Stewart Donner, Mulligan sat in the back seat. He was being extremely indecisive as he had to choose between life and money. He could put a bullet in Donner's head and recover the two hundred thousand or he could help the man escape the country and let him keep the cash. For someone who had been in the business for as long as he, this sort of morality based question could pose a serious problem.

The car took a turn and Mulligan saw a sign reading 'Wolf Lane'. He was about to arrive and had to make his decision. It was difficult, but in the end he decided that it would be best to let the man live and help him escape. He was fundamentally innocent after all. It's not like he had stolen the money or killed someone for it, the bribe had been a fair and just deal in which he had earned the money.

The Cadillac Sixteen pulled up and he got out. The first thing he did after that was light up a cigarette and observe the home. As he felt the nicotine and tobacco begin to enter his body, he saw that the house was at least half a century old. Probably the same house that the man grew up in as a child. It was painted a dull white and was two storeys high.

There was a small terrace on the first floor and a white Porsche Cayenne parked in the driveway. The expensive car made it clear to Mulligan that he wasn't the first one to have made an expensive deal with Donner.

After spending another minute standing, Mulligan finished the cigarette and stubbed it out. He then slowly walked towards the door and rung a golden doorbell. Minutes passed and then he rang the doorbell again. Could it be possible that the man wasn't home? Unlikely. His car still stood in the driveway.

Another minute or two passed and then the door swung open. Donner, who was dressed in a black tracksuit, was surprised to see Mulligan standing there and greeted him angrily, 'What the hell are you doing here?'

Mulligan took a deep breath and replied coolly, 'You're in danger. You need to get out of the country.'

Donner chuckled and asked skeptically, 'Really? Who's out to get me?'

Mulligan rolled his eyes. He was trying to help the man and wasn't even being taken seriously. 'Some people are out to get you for cancelling the dam project. They could have made a lot of money and are angry because you took away the opportunity.'

'Right. I'll take care of myself.' Donner then slammed the door shut.

Standing embarrassed by having the door slammed on his face, Mulligan was now angry. He pulled out his Model 500 revolver and kicked the door in. Seeing the door fall to the ground, Donner who was sitting on the couch, jumped up to his feet in fear. He was going to yell angrily, but changed his mind when he looked down the barrel of Mulligan's hand-cannon.

'I was only trying to help you. But now, you've left me with no choice.' Mulligan spoke in a reluctant tone.

Donner, who failed to understand what was going on, just stared back blankly.

Mulligan spotted the black money briefcase he had given Donner hidden behind the curtain and picked it up. Donner saw that his money was being stolen and asked, 'So that's what you wanted? The cash? Why did you tell me to leave the country then?'

Marvelling at the man's stupidity and ignorance, Mulligan answered by pulling the trigger. There was a loud sound as the bullet left the chamber and then entered Donner's skull. The power of the shot almost caused the man's head to explode as the body fell and landed on the couch. Mulligan felt guilty about what he had done but had no choice but to leave. He holstered his revolver and with the briefcase in hand he sprinted back to his car.

As the car drove away from the crime scene, Mulligan popped open the briefcase and counted the money. It was the full two hundred thousand. He felt excruciatingly guilty for what he had just done, but he knew he had no choice. If he hadn't put a bullet in Donner's head, then Hunt and the Cuban would have gunned him down instead. It was a simple matter of self-preservation.

When the Music's Over

Still hazy, Pym gathered all the strength he had to open his eyes. Sadly for him, he wasn't dreaming. He was still shirtless and bloody as he had been twenty minutes ago when he had passed out. His jaw was smashed and the pain from his shattered ribs was unimaginable. He was tied down to a chair, a metal one if he remembered correctly, with a tight rope around his wrists. Once again regaining his vision, he tried to study his environments, which would hopefully hold a clue to help him remember where he was.

He looked around and saw that it was an extremely dark room, much darker than he was comfortable with. The floors were a cold metal and so were the walls. He could hear his blood dripping onto the floor from his countless wounds. Ahead, there was a light. In all the literature he had ever read, a light represented a beacon of hope, but not in this case. The light showed him the silhouettes of two men, who he instantly recognized. The taller one stood with his hands in his pockets and stared down at him. The other one had a cigar in his mouth and seemed to be saying something.

Even after straining to listen, the two men remained inaudible. Realizing that he recognized the men, but couldn't remember their names meant something was wrong. Maybe his captors had made a mistake by smacking him too hard.

He then leaned back in his uncomfortable chair hoping to take advantage of the situation. The two men clearly hadn't noticed that he had recovered consciousness and maybe this would be the best time to get some rest and heal.

Unfortunately enough, that didn't happen. Jonathan Pym was not that lucky a man.

The shorter man with the cigar, noticed his prisoner moving and then said to his friend, 'He's up.'

The two men then approached him and as Pym saw them close up, he remembered who his captors were and unfortunately enough, he also remembered why he was tied to a chair. The tall man was Michael Hunt while the shorter one was the Cuban. Hunt, who was dressed in a black suit and black shirt, seemed to just watch while the Cuban, whose grey suit had gone red with blood, seemed to be doing the dirty work.

Without saying or asking anything, the Cuban removed his cigar from his mouth and stubbed it out against Pym's cheek. The pain was unimaginable as the flesh burned off and Pym screamed loud enough to burst his own ear drums. Hunt's face remained indifferent as he watched the man screech in agony while the Cuban let out a satisfied smile. The man was clearly a sadist.

'I'm going to ask you one more time Mr Pym,' the Cuban spoke with a dangerous calm, 'Who did you help sabotage the dam project?'

As Pym recovered from agony, he ignored the question. A punch to his nose reminded him that that probably wasn't a good idea.

'Why do you think it was me who helped the saboteurs?' Pym spoke between heavy breaths. Breathing was becoming difficult as both his mouth and nose were filled with blood.

The Cuban reached into his coat and pulled out a Smith & Wesson Model 686 revolver. He then held it by the opposite end and smacked the butt across Pym's temple. Once again, the victim screamed in agony as his forehead busted open and even more blood poured out.

'I know it was you, Mr Pym, who took away our chance to make millions because you were the only one besides Mr Hunt and me who knew the details of the project.' The Cuban spun the revolver around his index finger as he spoke.

The fact was that the Cuban was right. Pym had been detected by the process of elimination. Now that he had been found guilty, there was no way that he was going to be allowed to live. So being the rational person that he was, it seemed to him that maybe giving the names of his fellow conspirators would be the best way to save himself from unimaginable agony and be blessed with the sweet escape of a quick death.

'It was Mulligan and his men, from the Royal Citizen's Bank. They would have lost the lead if the project had gone through so they bribed Donner to prevent it from going through.' Pym finished speaking and then leaned back. Murmuring a short prayer, he closed his eyes. He was ready for the inevitable fate of every man.

The Cuban lifted up his gun and pointed it at his victim's face. He then looked towards Hunt for confirmation and got the go-ahead through a slight nod. Letting out a slight smile, the Cuban pulled the trigger and watched with sociopathic joy as the bullet entered Pym's skull and his head burst into a fountain of blood.

He then tucked his gun into his jacket and started walking back to his car with Hunt accompanying him. They were in a warehouse in the lower city that had been purchased for conducting activities of exactly this fashion. The damp and metallic structure that the two men were walking out of had been home to countless tortures, murders and mutilations. The drug business was not a pretty one.

As they approached the Cuban's newly purchased maroon-red Rolls Royce Ghost, Hunt asked coolly, 'So what are we going to do about this?'

The Cuban reached into his pocket and pulled out a cigar. He lit it as he contemplated the other man's question and after a few drags, he answered, 'Nobody messes with me and lives to talk about it. I want to take out Mulligan and all of his top men. Give me a list as soon as you can.'

Hunt let out a wide grin. He had wanted to do this for a long time, but hadn't been able to take any action because of Don Ponzarelli. The Cuban, however, was too powerful for even the Don to go up against. After all that Mulligan had done to harm him, there was finally going to be reckoning.

The next morning, the Cuban sat in his villa dressed in a dark green suit and black shirt. In his hand he held a piece of paper that was deadlier than most weapons. It was a hit list that Hunt had given him as per his request.

It read:

1. W. Mulligan
2. J. Wolfenstein
3. L. Lapidus
4. D. Caesar

Caesar stood outside the Sicilian Fountain restaurant. He calmly lit a cigarette. After getting out of a hectic meeting with a client who had nothing but complaints, a smoke served as an easy way to release tension. He was dressed in a grey suit and white shirt with brown leather shoes. He enjoyed the calm breeze and the hot weather. He almost felt as though he lived in a world without worries.

His hopes and dreams were quickly shattered as a black sedan pulled up right in front of him and a man dressed in a black suit got out. He had on black aviators and a white shirt making it difficult to identify any distinguishing features. What made the man an almost instant threat was the Heckler & Koch HK33 Assault Rifle that he carried under his arm. Pointing it straight at Caesar, the gunman pulled out down the trigger and instantaneously, a barrage of bullets decimated the area.

Fortunately having a quick reaction time, Caesar jumped down onto the pavement where he had protection behind parked cars. Never had he felt such gratitude for people who were parked in illegal spots. The drop to the ground had been too fast to successfully stop and, therefore, he even scraped a bit of his cheek on the rough ground.

The gunman reloaded his weapon and continued to approach his target. Knowing that if he wanted to live he would have to run, Caesar jumped up and began sprinting down the block. Behind him, the gunman fired off another entire clip, which miraculously missed Caesar and littered the building wall behind him with holes.

Quickly turning a corner, Caesar continued to run. The gunman sprinted after him, but was unsuccessful in attempting to shoot him while running. The HK33 wasn't that light a weapon after all. Caesar turned into an alley and pulled out his phone. He then speed-dialled Mulligan and hoped with all his heart that his boss would pick up.

As he continued to run while hearing the monotone ringing of the phone, Caesar temporarily forgot how close the chasing man had come. The gunman was clearly the fitter one. The call was answered and Caesar heard Mulligan's voice on the other end say, 'What's going on?'

'Help,' screamed Caesar before he dropped the phone. The gunman had unleashed another round of bullets and this time the target had been hit. Caesar had taken a shot in the back of his left shoulder, but that wasn't enough to keep him from running.

The gunman was beginning to get annoyed with this silly game of tag and decided on a more tactical approach. As the chase turned onto a long straight alley, Caesar picked up speed in order to survive the next incoming hail of gunfire. The gunman, however, decided on a different approach and quickly got down on one knee and then took three seconds to calmly aim his gun.

Caesar reached the end of the straight alley and just as he was about to take a turn, a single shot was fired from the assault rifle. The bullet went straight through the target's neck and Caesar hit the pavement with a thud. As he used both his hands to cover the wound, he shivered in fear of his almost inevitable death. The gunman holstered the massive assault rifle and slowly walked towards the dying man.

As he stood looking over at his victim with disgust, the gunman pulled out his sidearm, a Beretta M9 and aimed it at Caesar's head.

'Please don't,' Caesar managed to speak even though he was on the verge of death from blood loss.

The gunman chuckled at his victim's last attempt of self-preservation and then pulled the trigger. Since the gun was not silenced like the assault rifle had been, there was a loud bang as Caesar's brains were splattered across the floor of the god-forsaken alley.

The gunman, who was satisfied with his work, calmly walked back towards his black Porsche Panamera and got into the front seat. He threw his assault rifle onto the seat next to him and calmly began driving away. When he felt that the distance between him and his victim was enough, he pulled out his phone and dialled for his boss, the Cuban.

'What is it?' answered the Cuban in a heavy accent.

'I got the first one,' informed the gunman.

'Good job. Now go after the rest Manolo.' The Cuban then hung up.

Manolo had been a hitman for the Cuban for over seven years now. He had killed dozens of people for his boss and over the years he had realized one thing; in a city where the police are owned by the criminals, the best way to ensure a kill was to be the man with the bigger gun. And for that reason only, Manolo had spent a large amount of his earnings setting and stocking up a large collection of weapons. The favourite one, however, would always be the custom-silenced HK33.

Lapidus was driving in his Aston Martin Rapide when a black Porsche Panamera pulled alongside him. Both cars moved in almost a pre-synchronized parallel motion with the Aston Martin doing everything it could to break the layout. Neither braking nor accelerating helped. Nudging the car was out of the question as the body repairs would cost a fortune. Finally giving up, the car pulled up and Porsche stopped alongside it.

Getting out of his car with an annoyed look on his face, Lapidus raised his arms up into the air and barked, 'What the hell are you doing?'

Manolo got out of the Porsche with the HK33 in hand

and smiled at Lapidus. Realizing that there was something wrong, Lapidus studied the man and was surprised when he saw him carrying a massive gun. Quickly turning around, he began getting into his car when the gunman opened fire on the vehicle itself. The Aston Martin was ridden with bullets from head to toe with all the glass shattered including the head and tail lights.

Lapidus, who was crouched right outside the driver's side of the car, pulled out his Colt Anaconda. He knew he had to make his shots count because unlike the assault rifle, his gun could only hold a maximum of six bullets at a time. He rose from behind the car and quickly fired two shots in the general direction of his foe.

Both rounds from the revolver missed the target by a large distance as Manolo had moved away and was now approaching his target from the rear of the Aston Martin. Seeing the beautiful and elegant vehicle torn apart, Manolo almost felt a sense of regret. That moment of conflicting emotion, however, didn't even make him hesitate as he once again took aim at Lapidus and unloaded another clip of thirty bullets.

Knowing that he would have to play this smart, Lapidus waited for the other man to start reloading when the time came, he fired two more rounds from his Colt Anaconda. Both rounds once again missed their target by a pitiful distance. Seeing the other man's failure with firearms, Manolo chuckled and once again moved slightly closer to his target. Taking careful aim, he fired an entire clip. Lapidus, however, managed to survive by ducking under the car and as soon as the clip ran out, he quickly got out from hiding and sprinted across the street and into a supermarket.

What the target had done was annoying, but Manolo knew

how to deal with it. He threw his assault rifle back into his Porsche and drew out his M9 pistol instead. After screwing on a silencer onto the handgun, he walked across the street and entered the crowded supermarket. He would have to be extremely careful as the place was full of people and children of all ages right from teenage boys to mother's with their infant children.

Quietly walking around with his pistol at the ready, Manolo scouted the market looking for Lapidus. Several young boys saw the silenced pistol in his hand, but they wouldn't dare say anything. Checking the area isle by isle, Manolo knew he had to persevere to achieve his objective. His target could be absolutely anywhere after all.

After entering the market, Lapidus ran all the way to the end and ducked down behind the energy-drink refrigerator. He had two bullets left and he was going to have to make sure that they put down the man who was hunting him. He waited patiently with the gun at the ready, but knew that it might be a while before the man he was looking for actually came around.

After checking the last isle, Manolo saw the energy-drink refrigerator at the far end. Without even considering other options, he knew that this would be the place where his target would have hidden. To know such things without doubt is what made him good at his job. Seeing that there was no one else in immediate view, he brought up his pistol in front of him and took aim.

Lapidus knew that there was someone nearby as he heard solemn footsteps on the marble floor slowly and steadily approach. Whether it was the assassin or not was something that would be impossible for him to determine without the risk of opening fire on an innocent.

To lure out his target, Manolo walked up close to the energy-drink refrigerator and kicked it hard. The massive ice-box tumbled over and Lapidus burst out from behind it in order to avoid being crushed. As he jumped out from hiding, he fired two rounds at the assassin but unfortunately enough, they missed. In return, Manolo had also fired a single silenced round, which had caught Lapidus in the thigh.

The man fell to the floor and once again brought up the revolver to aim at the assassin. He had a clear shot at his enemy's head and he pulled the trigger.

There was only a click. He had run out of bullets.

Manolo let out an evil smile and then got down on his knees maintaining steady eye contact with his target. He held the tip of the M9 against the man's cheek to avoid any attempts at escape, not that they would matter.

'Why are you doing this?' Lapidus asked. He wanted to know why he was being hunted.

Manolo continued to smile and replied with a thick Cuban accent, 'You pissed off Mr Ribera. There is a price to pay for that.'

Lapidus exhaled a deep breath and then asked, 'Is this about the Da...'

Manolo pulled the trigger.

He didn't like talking to people who were about to die. It was an exercise in futility.

Two days later, Mulligan sat in his office with Jimmy across him. Mulligan was in an extremely foul mood when he had called the kid in for a meeting. The information he had received had disturbed him to the core. Now that Jimmy sat across him, he found it difficult to gather the courage to say what needed to be said.

'James, I need to tell you something.' Mulligan had used 'James' instead of 'Jimmy'. That was never a good sign.

'What happened boss?' asked the kid cautiously.

'You know that Cuban? Antonio Ribera?'

'Yeah, the drug lord. We stopped him from building a dam.'

Mulligan took a breath and then said softly, 'Well, it turns out that he found out that it was us and now he wants blood. He already killed Lapidus and Caesar. He's probably coming after us next.'

A silent moment passed.

'Caesar's dead?' A tear rolled down the kid's eye. He had just lost one of his closest friends.

Mulligan nodded in return and then leaned back in his chair. He lit a cigarette and prayed to god that the Cuban would back down, because if he didn't, two more people were going to die.

Meanwhile, Manolo walked through the maze that was the interior of the villa. He had only been inside five or six times before and still had trouble making his way to the roof as that was where his boss conducted operations. He was feeling uncomfortable as he was unarmed and was dressed in a black suit and white shirt with black aviators as usual. His look made him blend in well and made it almost impossible for him to be identified in a line-up. He had done everything he could to ensure he looked like everyone else.

Arriving at the roof, Manolo found his boss standing in a beach shirt and swimming costume. The Cuban was on the edge of his roof hot-tub with a beer in one hand and a cigar in the other. When he saw that his trusty shooter had arrived, he welcomed him with open arms. After a friendly embrace, both men settled into comfortable chairs.

The Cuban took a drag from his cigar and then asked, 'So what's the situation?'

Manolo took a deep breath and replied, 'I've taken out two. I'll take care of the rest soon enough.'

'Is Mulligan dead?' the Cuban asked after a few seconds.

Manolo shook his head and hoped for the best. He knew that his boss really wanted these people dead and there would be repercussions for not executing his order.

Unusually enough, the Cuban wasn't angry and simply said, 'You have till tomorrow.'

Two hours later, Manolo drove his Porsche Panamera into the parking lot of the Royal Citizen's Bank. After parking, he got out of his car and walked around looking for a Chevrolet Camaro. He had been informed that his target was the apparent owner of the car. After walking around for a few minutes, he came across a black Cadillac Sixteen. It was a magnificent car and Manolo studied it for a few minutes. When the driver of the car, who was sitting on the hood, flashed him a look of disgust, however, Manolo decided to move on.

The open-air parking lot was largely divided into eight different lanes. The area was almost completely full with most vehicles being averagely priced sedans with the occasional gems like the Cadillac Sixteen. Some of the car's had chauffeurs who marked their territory very clearly by sitting on the hood of their car, often with a cigarette in their mouth. Manolo had come to resent smoking as he considered it to be a long and painful method for suicide. An ignorant way of looking at things, but the way he looked at them nonetheless.

Finally finding the Camaro that he was looking for, Manolo approached the back door and stood next to it casually. The light green colour of the car was definitely very attractive and almost distracting as Manolo attempted to study the lock on the back door. It wasn't too strong and after several minutes of fondling around with it, it jerked open and Manolo got into the back seat.

He ducked down into the foot area, an extremely uncomfortable way of hiding, but one that was better than most others. In his jacket he had his silenced M9, but it was a bit difficult to reach from this angle. Instead, he had a piano wire ready in his hands and planned to use it instead of the pistol. This way, there would be no blood and that would mean that it would take longer, much longer, before the body was discovered.

Now it was time to play the waiting game. It was four forty-five and since office hours finished at five, it would only be a short wait of fifteen minutes. If the target decided to stay and work overtime, however, certain unforeseen problems could possibly arrive.

Fortunately enough, that was not the case as Manolo watched Jimmy walk out of the building and enter the parking lot. He seemed to have forgotten where he had parked and it took him a good ten minutes to find his car.

Pulling out his key, Jimmy unlocked the front door of his car and got into the driver's seat. As Manolo had predicted, the target hadn't even looked towards the back seat. As the car was started, the assassin quickly rose from his hiding position and looped the piano wire around Jimmy's neck. The kid struggled and rattled around powerfully as Manolo pulled on the wire and strangled the life out of his victim. With all the resistance, Jimmy managed to turn on the stereo by bumping his knee into it. As the colour from the man's face drained away, 'Paint It Black' by The Rolling Stones started playing. Another minute later, there was no struggling at all. James Wolfenstein was dead.

Driving around the roads of the upper city, Manolo considered different ways to go after Mulligan. The man was supposed to be excessively dangerous after all, and it would be best to think of a way where the risk for retaliation was minimal. Coming up with such a scenario, however, was almost as hard as implementing the kill. It took a good one hour to figure out, but Manolo knew what he had to do.

Mulligan sat in his office the next day. Tears flowed through his eyes as he held the autopsy reports of three of his people. He was drenched neck-deep in self-blame with the only thought flowing through his mind being that it was his fault that these people had died.

He scrolled slowly through morgue photos. Taking in every gruesome wound, whether it was a gunshot or a strangle mark. The wound on Caesar's neck had been caused by a powerful gun, something much bigger than a pistol and a revolver. That mystery gun scared him. It was difficult to face an unknown enemy.

Interrupting his thought process, the phone buzzed.

'Sir, I have an envelope for you.' The secretary maintained her acute professionalism.

'Bring it in please.' Mulligan spoke weakly.

After putting down the phone, a moment passed and then the door swung open. The secretary entered and placed a black envelope on the table and then vacated the room. The envelope had no posting on it, only printed white text on the top of it reading *William Mulligan*.

Mulligan carefully opened the letter and pulled out the

small piece of paper that lay within. It was yellow with plain black text imprinted onto it.

I will butcher you just as I have butchered your friends.

The message was simple, but carried a deep significance. It psychologically damaged Mulligan while at the same time encouraged him to ready himself to face what was coming. The Cuban had made it clear that Mulligan would not survive, not after preventing him from making millions of dollars.

Mulligan pulled out his lighter and lit one end of the note. As the flame began to grown and consume the rest of the parchment, he threw it into the trashcan. He then opened his drawer and pulled out his dual AMT Long-Slide Hardballer pistols and placed them in his jacket. The Model 500 revolver was useless against whatever heavy-weapon the assassin was going to carry. At least the Hardballers would give him a fighting chance.

At eleven that night, Mulligan stepped out onto the porch of the Royal Citizen's Bank. There were a few sparse cars parked around in the parking lot and there was relatively no one in sight. Suddenly, he saw his driver running towards him.

'Someone slashed the car's tires.' The driver spoke as he gasped for breath.

Twenty metres away, there was a silenced gunshot from the HK33. The bullet hit the driver in the head and the man dropped to the floor. Seconds later, a pool of blood began forming around him. Mulligan grew angry; this had been another unnecessary death. It started raining. Standing over the dead body of his loyal driver, he lit a cigarette. It would be best to calm down before the shooting began.

It took him about a minute to finish and then he stubbed

out the cigarette. As soon as the flame on the bud went out, Mulligan pulled out his pistols. It was time to finish this once and for all.

Manolo, who was ducked behind the Cadillac Sixteen a little distance away, opened fire first. He emptied the entire clip aiming at Mulligan, but not a single bullet hit the target. Mulligan had sprinted away and now hid behind one of the pillars on the porch. As Manolo began to reload, Mulligan ran towards cover, closer to the assassin. He had short range weapons so it would be best to reduce the gap.

After popping in the new clip, Manolo once again took aim at his target. It was difficult to get a clear shot as the man was well hidden. Mulligan, however, made it easier as he peeked out for a split second to fire off a couple of rounds from his pistols. His shooting was quite accurate and one of the bullets struck Manolo in his knee. After stumbling to the floor and attempting to ignore the agonizing pain of his wounded knee, Manolo took aim at Mulligan once again and fired of his entire clip. This attempt was more successful than the previous one as one of the rounds grazed Mulligan's cheek and left a deep wound.

As Manolo began to reload again, Mulligan jumped over the car and ran under the cover of the rain to closer cover. During his sprint he fired off a couple of rounds towards his enemy, but the randomly aimed shots didn't hit anything. Manolo finished reloading and then realized his enemy's strategy. Mulligan wanted to close as much distance as he could while Manolo reloaded so that he could be in range for a kill-shot.

Taking careful aim once again, Manolo fired off an entire clip. The car behind which Mulligan was taking cover was

obliterated. Following his plan, Mulligan jumped from cover and ran towards the assassin. This time, however, Manolo was prepared. Instead of reloading his assault rifle, he pulled out his pistol from his jacket and took a clear shot.

As Mulligan was running through the rain, he had no cover and therefore no chance. The well-aimed bullet from the pistol hit him right in the heart and the man stopped dead in his tracks. He dropped to his knees and then finally onto the floor.

Lying on the ground of the parking lot, Mulligan felt the rain gently fall on his face. With his last dying breath, he managed to say 'I hope they have cigarettes in hell.'